Witching on a Star

Star

Erin Bedford

Witching on a Star © 2018 Embrace the
Fantasy Publishing, LLC

Also by Erin Bedford

The Underground Series
Chasing Rabbits
Chasing Cats
Chasing Princes
Chasing Shadows
Chasing Hearts

The Mary Wiles Chronicles
Marked by Hell
Bound by Hell
Deceived by Hell
Tempted by Hell

Starcrossed Dragons
Riding Lightning
Grinding Frost
Swallowing Fire
Pounding Earth

The Celestial War Chronicles
Song of Blood and Fire

Crimson Fold
Until Midnight
Until Dawn
Until Sunset

Curse of the Fairy Tales
Rapunzel Untamed

Her Angels
Heaven's Embrace
Heaven's A Beach

Granting Her Wish
Vampire CEO

Witching On A Star

Erin Bedford

Chapter 1

THERE IT WAS, STARING at me. Bulbous, red, and angry. It was the very definition of my immediate doom, and it taunted me.

"Maxine!" my mom's voice shouted up the stairs. "We're going to be late if you don't hurry it up."

I turned away from the mirror where a pimple that had chosen today of all days to find a home in the middle of my forehead bulged out. "I'll be down in a minute. I'm having an existential crisis!"

"A zit is not a crisis. Being late to your own graduation is a crisis."

Not bothering to argue with her, I shot another glare at the horrible zit before rearranging my blonde hair so that it swept across my forehead, semi-hiding the red bump. Letting out an exasperated huff, I spun back to my bed where my graduation dress laid.

Shrugging out of my jeans and t-shirt, I swapped my bra for a strapless one that would go with my halter dress, hooking the strap around my neck. I picked up the garment and stepped into the pale pink dress, the material smooth and slinky against my skin.

"There's my little valedictorian," my mom said as she popped her head into my room.

I spun around, clutching the dress to my chest. "Mom! Knock. It's called knocking!"

My mom snorted and rolled her eyes, moving further into my room. "Not like I haven't seen it all before. I gave birth to you, you know."

My face scrunched up in disgust. "Ew, mom. I don't need a visual." I busied my hands with tying my dress up and started searching for my shoes.

Chuckling at my distress, my mom took a seat on the edge of my bed, her pale blue eyes - the same color of my own - squinting in my direction. "I don't see this elusive zit you are so upset about."

Happy that I had successfully hidden the malicious mound of flesh determined to ruin my graduation, I grinned. "If you can't see it, then I'm not going to show you."

She gave me a look that caused me to groan. I knew what was coming. The I-know-what's-best-for-you look always starts a lecture about …

"Have you been doing your yoga?" She raised a brow, her face far too young to have a teenage daughter, her soon to be a high school graduate daughter.

"Yes, mom," I drew out with a growl. "I do it every morning and evening."

"Well," - my mom clicked her tongue as she adjusted the ponytail of her blonde hair - "if you were doing them like you should, then you wouldn't be getting zits."

My mom liked to think that yoga cured everything, from daily facial issues to curing cancer. But even though she had her own special adjustments to the usual yoga positions, I found it a bit farfetched to think stretching could change my life. Still, I did them rigorously, you know, just in case.

"Mom, I've been doing them, but not even daily stretches and meditation can overcome the stress of having three hundred students and their friends and family staring at you while you speak about what the future has in store for you." My voice went up a few pitches during my semi-rant, leaving me out of breath by the end of it.

Standing, my mom gestured toward me. "Come, show me what you're doing."

I shook my head and sagged. "Mom, I know what I'm doing. I've only been doing them since I was three."

She gave me a perturbed look. "Obviously you are doing something wrong, or you wouldn't be so stressed out. Now, come on. Show me Power pose one."

Power pose was just an altered name for Warrior one. Why she bothered to change the name when it looked exactly the same, I couldn't fathom, but now wasn't the time to bring it up. I shifted my stance so that my right foot was pointing ninety degrees to the right and my left foot was forty-five degrees to the right. Bending my front leg, I reached my arms up, stopping at the chest rather than going all the way to the sky like the real Warrior one would have required.

"There." I held the pose and met my mom's gaze. "Satisfied?"

Circling me, my mom looked over my stance with a critical eye. She stopped before me and stared at my hands. Reaching out, she adjusted the placement of my fingers aligned together, pushing them up to my heart. "It's not just about the position, it's about the purpose behind it. You must focus your energies. Breath into the ball of light inside of you."

Ball of light. Pfft. My mom was always referring to some great light inside of me. The source of my power. Whatever that meant. Not wanting to fight with her, I closed my eyes and tried to do as she instructed.

Focus. I am focused. Centered. The light in me is full of calm, peace, and exuberant. Despite all my mental instructions, the light in my mind's eye was anything but a docile lamb. It jerked with internal chaos, spikes of pure light jolting out in every direction. The power of it became so bright that I squinted even with my eyes closed.

"You're grimacing. Why are you grimacing?" my mom asked me, frustration clear in her voice.

"I'm not grimacing. I'm focusing," I lied as the ball of light grew bigger and brighter. I clasped my hands tighter in front of me. A static shock ran through my hands, causing me to gasp and open my eyes.

"What is it?" My mom's face furrowed in worry, her hands going for mine, but I pulled away staring down at them.

"I don't know." I frowned. I'd never felt anything like that before. I'd always thought of the big ball of light as a Mister Miyagi sort of metaphor, not anything real. But I knew I hadn't imagined the shock that even now made my fingers tingle. My eyes moved from my hands to my mom's concerned gaze, and I forced a smile. "Just freaking myself out. I'm sure it's nothing."

My mom didn't look convinced but didn't ask further. One thing I loved about her was that she wasn't like other moms. She didn't push me for more than I wanted to give. She'd always been the kind to let me come to her.

"Alright, but you need to hurry up, or you won't be able to get pictures beforehand like you wanted." My mom pointed at me as she made for the door.

I nodded and then waited for the sound of her going down the stairs before looking back at my hands. Had that really happened? Or was I just too stressed out by graduation? It wasn't like I hadn't had my share of shocks before but nothing like this. Usually, they were from touching metal or an electrical outlet, not from my own body.

My phone buzzed, breaking me out of my mental assessment. Shaking my head and smiling, I picked up my phone and read the message waiting for me.

Callie: Two hours and counting!! Are you ready to be free of this hell hole?

I grinned at my best friend's message. Callie always could be a bit overdramatic. High school hadn't been that bad. We weren't in the popular crowd by any means, but we also didn't lack for friends. Calling Central High School a hell hole was going a bit far.

Me: Ready for college. The libraries will be beyond comparison.

Almost immediately, I got a response.

Callie: Only you would be thinking with your big brain rather than about all the wild parties and hotties waiting for us at Brown.

Callie and I had both gotten accepted into our Ivy League school of choice. It had taken some fighting with my mom and dad to get them to agree to let me go so far away from them. Rhode Island was quite a bit away from Atlanta, Georgia, and my parents and I had a really close relationship. It would be hard for me as well as them.

I quickly texted Callie back that I'd see her at graduation and then finished getting ready. It only took me a few minutes to splash on some eyeshadow, mascara, and eyeliner. I grabbed my favorite strawberry lip balm and smeared it over my lips, giving them a shiny pink color. After that, I scanned over myself in the full-length mirror once more. Bra straps concealed. Hair bouncing and lively. Zit successfully concealed. With a satisfied nod, I headed for the door.

Bounding down the stairs, I heard my mom's voice in the kitchen, her words making me pause.

"I don't know how much longer we can keep this from her, Wesley. My spell is starting to fade. She's already stronger than I was at that age."

My dad's voice sounded reassuring. "Patty, I'm sure everything will be fine. You've done an excellent job of protecting her. Maybe it's time to start letting her take care of herself."

"But Headmistress McClain keeps sending notices, wanting to know if Max will be joining them," she retorted. "I can't keep stalling. She's going to Brown soon."

Not wanting to get caught eavesdropping as well as wanting an explanation, I continued down the stairs and popped around the corner to where they sat at the kitchen island. "Protect me from what?"

My mom and dad both started, their hands clasped together. My mom gave me a weak smile that wasn't at all convincing. "From the horrors of college life, of course."

"Your mom's just a bit nervous about our baby moving away from home." My dad chuckled and wrapped an arm around my mom. Most people had a challenging time thinking Wesley Norman was my dad. Not

14

only because he was super famous - in the archeology world anyway - but because we look nothing alike. While my mom and I were run of the mill blonde-haired, blue-eyed Nordics, my father's brown skin and almond-shaped eyes screamed his Egyptian inheritance. I used to agonize over not getting his exotic features but long ago came to love my own features. I did have his lips, bowed and more expressive than I cared for.

Lifting a brow, I said, "Really? I'm not a little kid. I'm eighteen."

"Barely," my dad pointed out, picking up his coffee cup and pointing it at me before taking a long drink.

I rolled my eyes. "I'm legally an adult, I'll be fine. Plus, Callie will be there."

My mom snorted.

"What's wrong with Callie?" I asked, cocking my head to the side. "You've never had a problem with her before."

I moved over to the island and shifted through the mail. My eye caught something with my name on it. A blue and green shield with a scroll and owl decorated the corner of the envelope. Winchester Academy. Another school wanted me, no doubt. I'd gotten about a dozen or so letters like that in the last month. I never opened them. I had my heart set on Brown, and that was that.

"There's nothing wrong with Callie," my mom explained, taking the mail from me and handing me a banana. "But she doesn't exactly have her mind set on her academic future."

"She got into Brown, same as me," I reminded her, before taking a bit of the banana. "She's just as smart as the rest of them." My mom gave me a look, and I shrugged. "So, she's a bit boy crazy. Who isn't at our age?"

My dad cleared his throat.

"Okay, I'm not exactly the same as all those hormonally charged teens that I grew up with, but I can't help that." I frowned and took another bite of my banana. "None of the guys at our school has ever really interested me. They're all so …" I trailed off, unable to find the right word.

"Immature?" my mom supplied.

I shook my head.

"Full of shit?" my dad inserted, making me smile.

"Yes, but not quite what I was going for. I don't know." I sighed dramatically. "I just want magic in my life. You know that spark that sets him apart from all the others. Like you guys have."

My mom and dad exchanged a loving look before both of their phones buzzed. They both grabbed their phones at the same time as I finished my banana.

"That's the museum," my dad grumbled, typing away on his phone. "They want me to come in to do some paperwork for my last expedition."

"No," my mom told him, looking up from her phone. "This is your daughter's big day. Tell them they can wait until Monday." She typed a quick message into her phone before grabbing her purse off the other counter. "That was Maggie's mom. She wanted to know if I would be chaperoning tonight's party. I thought you told all your friends about tonight?"

We headed for the door as I answered. "I did. It's not my fault some of my friends have less trusting parents than I do."

My mom gave me a soft smile. "Well, not all teenagers are as open and honest with their parents as you are."

I grinned broadly.

"Maggie?" my dad started, climbing into our red Ford Explorer. "That's the one who crashed her car into the lake, right?"

Shaking my head, I giggled. "No, that was Jessica. Maggie is the one who got caught having a coed sleepover for her sixteenth birthday."

"Oh, right." My dad turned the ignition and then leaned over his seat to look at me in the back. "She's not going to Brown too, is she?"

This time, I laughed even harder. "With her grades? Maggie would be lucky to get into community college. She spent most of the senior year exploring the football team's anatomy than anything else."

My dad let out a sigh. "Good."

My mom and I exchanged a grin. I loved my dad, but he could be such a ... well, dad. Thank God I wasn't some serial dater like my friends. I'd had exactly three relationships if you could call high school boyfriends relationships.

There was Jake in eighth grade, who was too scared to say the word nipple let alone try to touch one. In tenth grade, I had a five-month relationship with a foreign exchange student named Clause who showed me why they called it French kissing. Then there was ...

"At least that Jaron boy won't be anywhere near you," my dad continued as we made our way to the convention center.

"Wes." My mom gave him a warning look before shooting a sympathetic smile my way.

"It's okay, mom." I shifted in my seat uncomfortably. "It's not like I can't talk about it."

"I know, honey, but it's okay to be upset. I would be too." She reached back and patted my knee.

It wasn't like I wasn't upset. Like my mom said, I had every right to be. Jaron had been my only long-term relationship, spanning through most of the eleventh grade until a few weeks ago when he announced he'd be going to college on the other side of the country. That parting wouldn't have been so bad had he not decided we shouldn't try to do a long-distance relationship the morning after prom. Oh, yeah. Where he had just deflowered me. Right. It's fine. Completely fine.

That light flashed in my head once more, and my fingers buzzed. I sat on them for good measure, not wanting to deal with whatever freaky thing going on with my body today.

It was just stress, I reminded myself as we pulled into the convention center. I only had a few hours left until I would never have to see him ever again. I'd be on my way to Brown and a new magical future.

I tried to keep my positivity up as we parked and climbed out of the car. After we entered the convention center, I hugged my parents and made my way over to where the students were supposed to gather and collect our gowns.

Telling Mr. Oliver, the science teacher, my name, I took my gown and started to put it on over my clothes. Just as I was about to zip it up, a piercing scream filled my ears, about breaking my eardrums.

"Max!" Callie wrapped her arms around me and jumped up and down, thoroughly shaking my insides up. "Can you believe it?"

Pushing at her hands but unable to hide my grin, I replied, "I'd believe it more if I could hear."

Callie dropped her arms. "Oops, sorry. I'm just so excited! We'll be heading to Brown in a few short months and then it's Rhode Island hotties for everyone."

Grinning as I pinned my cap to my head, I asked, "Is there really a difference between Rhode Island hotties and Georgia hotties?"

My best friend's brown eyes widened, her mouth dropping open like I'd just announced my alliance with Adolf Hitler. "Are you kidding me? The Rhode Island hotties are way better than Georgia hotties. I mean, they're sophisticated and have those northern accents. They shouldn't even be allowed in the same sentence as these wannabe hotties." She brushed a hand off

20

toward some of the male students. My eye focused on one male student in particularly.

Jaron stood with his back to me, his gown already on and his cap covering the tight black curls on his head. He laughed at something his friends said, making his broad shoulders shake. I'd been in love with him once. Or at least, I thought I was. Now, it hurt just to look at him. A petty part of me wanted him to feel the burn of rejection the same way I did.

That light in my head froze up for a moment before becoming even more chaotic.

"Do you smell smoke?" Callie asked, knocking me out of my daze.

I sniffed the air and did smell something burning. A familiar voice cried out, and my eyes jerked back to Jaron, who was fighting to get the robe off, the edge of it set ablaze. My eyes widened, and my heart beat rapidly in my chest. Had I done that? I'd been thinking about burning, and then he suddenly caught on fire like that? It had to be a coincidence, right? Something inside me that had been off all day told me that it wasn't. Not at all.

Chapter 2

THE ROAR OF APPLAUSE filled my ears as I finished my speech. I didn't know how I got through it. Or how I even remembered what I said with the shock of what happened to Jaron.

They were able to get the fire out before my ex-boyfriend was burned to a crisp. Sadly, his robe did not make it. The teachers figured Jaron was smoking a cigarette which got too close to his robe. This caused him to get into big trouble as well as keeping him from walking with the rest of us.

I wanted to step up for him. I knew without a doubt that Jaron would never smoke. His grandfather had died of lung cancer. Smoking was abhorrent to him. But what was I going to say? His robe spontaneously combusted because I was thinking about burning him for hurting me?

Yeah, that would go over well.

I barely managed to walk off the stage and take my place with the other students without tripping over my own feet. No one seemed to notice though, they were all too caught up in the day, getting their diploma and moving on with their lives. Only Callie gave me a curious look of concern, but even that didn't last when they started calling our names.

As they started to name off the names, my mind whirled once more with what happened to Jaron. I never really wanted to hurt him. I certainly wouldn't have set him on fire if given a choice. So, why did it happen? Was there something wrong with me?

Soon, they were calling my name and somehow, I walked toward the stage. I climbed the stairs once more and took my diploma. I didn't stop to take pictures but kept walking toward the other side of the stage and right out the side door. I knew my mom was going to get me for it later, but I really just needed to get some air.

There was a flutter of voices behind me as I raced out of the auditorium and then out of the convention center. When I saw the sky, I quickly pulled in gasps of air. Usually, in this kind of crisis, I would get into Child's pose which involved me sitting on the ground, but concrete and dresses don't really mesh well.

Instead, I did the second-best thing, a standing forward bend.

Clasping one arm over the other, I bent forward so that my top half was hanging in the air. I took slow deep breaths in through the nose and out through my mouth, praying to whoever may be listening to help me.

I'm not insane. It was a coincidence. The teachers were right, someone was smoking.

Even as I tried to sell it to myself, I knew it was a lie. Too many things had happened today for it to be just a coincidence. But if it wasn't, then what happened? Was I telekinetic? No, that didn't sound right. I haven't moved anything with my mind lately. I also couldn't read people's minds. Thankfully, that ruled out telepathy. I had to be some kind of mutant breed. How else did I explain what happened?

Before I could get too much into my evaluation of my mutant genes, the door to the convention center burst open behind me. "Max!" my mom called out and then sighed. "Oh my God, there you are. I was so worried. What's wrong? Why'd you run out like that?"

I jerked up from my forward bend, a mistake I quickly paid for as the wave of vertigo took over. A hand held my shoulder, keeping me from falling over. I closed my eyes and centered myself. When I felt like I would topple over, I turned to my mom.

"I'm sorry to worry you." I offered her a small smile. "I just got a bit overwhelmed by it all. You know the graduation, finally leaving for college. It all kind of caught up with me."

My mom believed the lies I was spewing and gave me an understanding smile before pulling me into her arms. "Oh, honey, I understand. I was where you were not too long ago. It'll be hard, leaving one life to start another. But at least you have your family to help you through it. I didn't have that."

My lips pursed together at the mention of my grandparents. I'd never met my mom's parents. They never agreed to mom marrying my dad, and so they never wanted to be a part of our lives. Even when I was born, they stayed away. I never missed them though. I had dad's parents to fill the void of grandparents. They spoiled me rotten too.

Thinking of them made my heart swell, and some of the anxiety faded away. While we were hugging, the ceremony must have finished because out poured my graduating class and their friends and family. I held onto my mom, just basking in her embrace while the crowd of people swarmed around us.

My mom had always been my touchstone. No matter how bad things got I always knew she could make it better, but for some reason, I couldn't bring myself to tell her what happened with Jaron. I knew she would love me no matter what, but how did you explain what I suspected without sounding like a crazy person? It wasn't until my dad came out with Callie in tow did I release mom.

"Hey Max," Callie wrapped her arms around me, pulling me against her side. "Where'd you go? You missed Patrick Zelken flash the entire auditorium." She giggled and swayed us back and forth.

"Alright, ladies." My dad held up his camera. "Let's get a few pictures so we can get out of this madhouse."

For a moment, holding onto Callie with a big grin on my face as my dad clicked away on his camera, everything was perfect. All the weirdness from the day faded away into the back of my mind. It was just a singular perfect moment. The kind that only happens once in a lifetime and shouldn't be taken for granted. And I didn't plan to miss a single second.

I had that same mindset a few hours later when we were back at my house. Music blared from the speakers, and half of my graduating class tried to cram into my parent's four-bedroom house. Thankfully we had a big enough backyard for the overspill, or our house might have exploded from so many teens.

"Callie!" I shouted over the music, holding my cup up. "I'm going to get something to drink."

Callie nodded as she danced with one of her crushes - of which she had many - and I headed toward the kitchen. I fought my way through the hoard of hormones until I got to the cooler of sodas. My parents were laid back enough to let me have a graduation party but not so much to let a bunch of minors drink alcohol on their property. That was just asking for trouble. I'd never been much into drinking in any case, and everyone seemed to be having fun without their brains being turned to chemical-filled mush.

I popped the top of my soda and tilted my head back. The cool liquid coated my throat and stimulated my already sugar-high brain. Someone tapped on my shoulder. I turned around, my soda can still poised at my lips.

When Jaron's face came into view, I suddenly forgot how to swallow. Sputtering and hacking up soda, I slammed the can onto the counter. Jaron patted me on the back, helping me to get my lungs working again.

"You okay?"

I wiped my eyes with the back of my hand and nodded. "Yeah, sorry. You startled me." I glanced down at my feet before looking back at him. "I thought you weren't coming?"

Jaron rubbed the back of his head, a sheepish look on his face. "Well almost dying kind of puts things into perspective. I didn't want to leave with any bad feelings between us."

The reminder of how Jaron had almost died killed any sugar buzz I might have had. It was my fault he'd almost died. I'd done it, and he was here to make nice with me.

"I'm sure it was terrifying," I forced out, trying to seem sympathetic when really my pulse could put a fighter jet to shame.

"Don't let this guy fool you," our classmate and Jaron's best friend Bryan threw an arm around Jaron's shoulders. "He was hardly fighting for his life. Maybe scorched a bit."

Jaron shook his head and shoved his friend away. "Don't try to play it down. You weren't the one on fire." Bryan rolled his eyes and then headed back into the party, leaving us alone again. Jaron met my gaze again and frowned. "Don't believe him. It was worse than you think. One minute I was standing there laughing with my friends and the next my robe is on fire, and I'm fighting for my life." He scoffed. "Mrs. Abernathy had the gall to think I was smoking. Me!"

I chuckled nervously. "Yeah, that's ridiculous."

"Exactly!" Jaron gestured a hand toward me and shook his head once more. "I still don't know how it happened. Some graduation prank maybe?"

I shrugged. "Maybe. Everyone was a bit hyped up." Unlike me, whose nerves were twisted so tight they could pop like a soda top.

Something like gunfire sounded, making everyone in the room freeze. My shoulders were up around my ears as my eyes widened. I searched the room for the perpetrator, but no following shots were fired. Someone turned down the music, and my dad ran into the kitchen.

"Is everyone okay?" he asked, his eyes wide. He found me and rushed to my side. "What happened?"

I shook my head. "I don't know. Jaron and I were just talking, and something sounded like it exploded."

"Hey! Not cool, man."

We all turned toward the guy talking. Eric something or another as he stood above the cooler.

"What is it?" my dad asked, moving over to his side. He looked down into the cooler, and the frown on his face deepened.

Not waiting for an explanation, I moved to my dad's side. My eyes widened at what I saw. All the cans in the cooler had exploded. Their tops popped clean off, and soda spewed from them quickly beginning to fill up the cooler.

Without a word, I raced out of the kitchen and bounded up the stairs. It happened again. I thought something, and it happened. There was no other explanation for it. It had to have been me again.

I slammed my bedroom door behind me, my hands going to my hair. Tugging on the roots, I paced my room. There had to be a logical explanation. There had to be. I was switched at birth and am really some space alien with abilities beyond human understanding.

Not helping.

Unlike outside the convention center, I could go into Child's pose. I'd already changed out of my dress into a pair of jeans and a tank top. No need to be prim and proper.

I dropped to my knees and practically threw my head to the ground. Breath. Just breath. It would be alright. No one knew it was me. Hell, I didn't even know it was me. As far as anyone knew it was just one freak accident after another ... that coincidentally happened when I was near.

Screwed. I was so screwed.

A knock on my door caused my head to pop up from the ground. My mom stuck her head around the door, concern pulling at her lips. "Honey, are you alright? Your dad said you bolted out of the kitchen in a hurry."

Sighing deeply, I sat back up. "No, mom. I'm not. There's something I need to tell you."

My mom's frown deepened, and she stepped into the room, closing the door behind her. Coming to sit beside me on the ground, she brushed my hair behind my ear. "What is it? You know you can tell me anything."

I smiled slightly. "That's just it. I'm not sure how to even tell you. Or if I'm just going crazy."

"I'm sure you're not crazy."

I glanced over at her and raised a brow. "You say that now but wait until I tell you—"

My bedroom door opened, and my dad stood in the doorway interrupting my admission. His eyes landed on my mom and me, and he quickly entered and closed the door once more. This time though, he locked it.

Strange.

"Don't want any nosy bodies coming to investigate," my dad explained with a goofy grin. He tucked his hands into his pockets and sat on the bed behind us. "So, what are we freaking about this week?"

"Maxine was just about to tell me," my mom told him, turning her expectant gaze back to me.

Taking a deep breath, I decided to just go for it. "I think I might be a mutant. Or at least some kind of alien life form," I spewed out all at once, making my words jumble together enough that I wasn't quite sure they even understood me.

For a moment, my mom and dad just stared at me, then they exchanged a look that I interpreted as they thought I was insane. What really nailed the head in the coffin was when they started laughing.

I scowled and wrapped my arms around my waist. "It's not funny. It's true." When they only laughed harder, I started to explain. "I caught Jaron's robe on fire at graduation from just thinking it. And, just now, I was thinking how I was wound tight enough to pop the top off a can and what happens?" I paused for dramatic effect. "All the cans in the cooler break open! I'm telling you, I'm a freak of nature."

"Honey," my mom chuckled and wiped a finger underneath her eye. "You're not a freak."

I growled and twisted around to face her. "Then how do you explain everything that happened? I'm not making this crap up. I really did cause those things to happen."

My mom lifted her hands in front of her. "I'm not saying you didn't. I believe you." She glanced at my dad and then grabbed his hand in hers. "We both do."

"Right." My dad nodded, no trace of humor left on his face.

"Okay, so if you believe me then why were you laughing at me?" I wiped my hands on my jeans, my hands sweaty from my admission.

Shaking her head, my mom smiled. "We weren't laughing at you, Max. We were laughing because you think you're some kind of alien."

"But how else do you explain ...?"

"Now we aren't saying aliens don't exist," my dad interrupted me. "God knows I've seen many things in my discoveries that point toward higher life forms, but we know for a fact you aren't one of those."

"Then I'm a mutant of some kind." I sighed and fell back onto the ground, staring up at the ceiling. "I'm going to be shipped off to some school for mutants where a bald guy in a wheelchair is going to help me control my powers, aren't I?"

"You're not a mutant." The audible sound of my mom's sigh made me pick my head up slightly.

"I'm not?"

"No, you're not." Mom shook her head and held a hand out. She twisted her wrist in some kind of fancy maneuver, and four books from my bookshelf came floating toward her, landing in a neat pile in her hand.

I gaped at her, sitting fully up once more. "What ... what? Hold the phone, you can do it too? You're a mutant too?" My eyes widened as I realized my whole life was a lie.

"We're not mutants," Mom growled, sending the books flying back to their spot on the bookshelf. "You're not an alien, a space being, or anything else you've read about in your science fiction books. You're a witch, Max. A witch. Just like me."

I blinked once and pointed a finger at myself. "I'm a witch."

"Yes."

"And you're a witch." I pointed the finger at her.

She nodded. "Yes."

"Are you a witch?" I asked my dad, who shook his head.

"Nope. Just an ordinary guy who fell in love with an extraordinary girl." He leaned forward to wrap an arm around my mom, and they exchanged a lovey-dovey look.

"Okay." I swallowed hard and moved my head up and down. "I can get behind this. I'm a witch. Okay, cool. So, can I do whatever I want then? Like, change my hair purple or teleport?"

Mom laughed. "No, not anything. You need to learn to control your powers before you can think about teleportation. Even then it's very tricky magic. And as far as coloring your hair purple, I wouldn't advise it. Beauty magic can be pretty complicated and, in some cases, permanent."

"So, how do I learn how to control it? Will you teach me?" I inched closer to her excitement taking over. Mom opened her mouth to answer, but I didn't let her get a word in edgewise. "Can we fly on brooms? Do we have to dance naked under the full moon? What about warts? I'm not going to get any of those, am I? Because I'm already struggling with acne. Though, I guess I could magic them away in any case—"

"Maxine!" my mom shouted my name cutting my round of questions off.

I ducked my head and gave an apologetic smile. "Sorry."

Letting out a deep breath, my mom shook her head. "I understand you're excited, but there are things you need to understand. Things you need to learn, and you can't learn those from me. Most of all ..." She paused and exchanged a look with my dad. "You have a decision to make. One that will change your life forever."

"Okay ...?" I drew out glancing between the two. "What is it?"

My mom leveled me with a serious look, the humor gone from her face. "Do you want to be a witch?"

"Uh ... is this a trick question?" My brows furrowed in confusion, my eyes darting from my dad to my mom as if one of them would say 'Gotcha!' at any moment. But neither of them did. "I'm not sure how to answer this. I mean, one part of me wants to jump up and down and scream that, of course, I want to be a witch, but the other half wants to know ... what's the catch?"

"The catch, as you say," my mom started, "is that you would have to go to a witch school to learn how to control your abilities like your grandparents and I did before me."

"Okay, that doesn't sound so bad." I shrugged, not really sure where she was going with it.

"What your mom isn't saying," my dad continued for her, "is that being a witch isn't like being a vegetarian. You can't hang out with the same people as you did before. You'd have to give up your life as a human. Which means ..."

"No Brown with Callie," I finished for him, my heart sinking. "But mom married you, and you're not a witch. She doesn't have any witch friends, right? You're just a New Age shop owner."

My mom pursed her lips, a sadness covering her face. "That was my choice. I chose to leave the magical community to be with your dad. Your grandparents disowned me because of it. That's why you never see them. And as far as magical friends? I still have a few, but it's hard. Certain rules have to be followed to be a witch. Rules that will make it impossible for you to keep your human friends."

Mom breathed deeply and grasped my hand. "What I'm trying to tell you, Max, is that if you choose to be a witch, you'll have to leave this life behind. Is that something you want to do?"

I was quiet for a moment, my mind whirling with all the additional information. The prospect of being a witch, of having this whole other side of me I never knew, was hard to give up just like that. I'd always been an academic type. Having a new world of possibilities opened up to me was every academic's dream. I wanted more than anything to pursue it.

Except ... what about Callie?

I voiced that very question to my parents.

My mom shrugged. "You can still talk to her, but you can't tell her you're a witch or anything about the magical community. Can you live with that secret? Never being able to open up completely to her again?"

"But you told dad," I pointed out. "Obviously, the rules were broken there."

My mom smiled sadly. "That's because he found out despite my best efforts, not because I told him."

Dad laughed. "I'll have to tell you sometime about how I figured it out. It's quite a story."

Mom gave him a look, shutting him up. "For a witch to marry outside of our kind isn't unheard of or forbidden, but they certainly make it hard to live with. It'll be easier to keep it from Callie if you're in different schools and who knows? Maybe you'll make a new best friend." She shrugged and offered me a soft smile.

Standing to her feet, my father followed her toward the bedroom door. "Why don't you think about it for a bit? But you'll need to decide soon. Winchester Academy is like any other college. You have to put in your response if you want to go."

"Okay," I said quietly, watching them leave, but my dad stopped at the door.

"Don't think of it as losing something, Max. Think of it as gaining a whole new part of your life that you didn't know you had. It could be quite an adventure."

I nodded, not answering. I understood what my dad was saying, but what I didn't know was if this adventure would be worth the costs.

Chapter 3

"IF I'VE BEEN A witch since birth, why did I only start showing my powers now?" I asked a few days later at breakfast. I grabbed a bowl and poured myself some cereal before scooping some into my mouth. "I mean, I didn't have an inkling of my magical abilities until graduation. Why then? Why now?"

My mom picked up her cup of coffee and moved over to sit in front of me at the kitchen table. "First, don't talk with your mouth full. Second, you didn't have powers because I put a spell on you."

I choked on my mouthful of cereal. "You what?"

Shrugging, my mom took a drink of her coffee. "I wanted you to have a normal human life. So, I put a spell on you to hide your powers. I was going to tell you this summer and let you decide for yourself, but then ..."

Suddenly the conversation I'd overheard the morning of graduation came back to my mind. "My powers got too big for your spell."

"Yeah."

Thinking about her words, I continued eating my cereal. Eventually, I noticed someone was missing. "Where's dad?"

Mom sighed. "At the museum. They're bugging him again about going on some exhibition over in the Middle East. I was hoping he'd have a little more time off before going off again."

I recognized the sadness in my mom's voice. My dad might be a big superstar to the archaeologist crew, but a lot of the time, that meant he had to be away for weeks, sometimes months at a time on a dig. My mom used to go with him, but when I was born, she chose to stay behind with me. I knew it put a strain on their relationship and always made me feel a little guilty.

"Well, why don't you go with him?" I asked, standing and putting my bowl in the sink.

"I can't do that." My mom shook her head though I could see the hopeful spark in her eyes.

"Sure, you can. I'm going off to school. There's no need for you to hang around here. You should be off having adventures of your own." I waved a hand in the air, trying to convince her.

"But I have the shop to think about and my students," she tried to argue. It was a halfhearted attempted I could tell.

I continued to try to convince her. "You have a manager, don't you? And I'm sure your students will understand."

My mom seemed to think on it for a moment and then she glanced over at me. "Why are we talking about what I'm going to do when we should be talking about you?"

I winced. She caught me. I'd been delaying my decision as much as I could. So much so that I'd been avoiding Callie as well. I didn't want her to think something was wrong, and I knew that if she asked me, I might spill everything.

"So, have you decided?" my mom lifted an expectant brow.

"No ... yes. I don't know." I sighed and flopped down into my seat again. "I want to go, I do, but I don't want to leave Callie."

"I understand." My mom nodded. "It's a hard decision."

That was putting it mildly. This was a monumental decision. Something that couldn't be decided on the fly. Or in a matter of a few days.

On the one hand, there was magic and a whole new world for me to explore. I would be one of the few people in the world allowed to access this phenomenal world, and I would be giving up a lot to pass on this chance.

However, there was a lot to say about being a human and living a human life. I've seen plenty of movies and read a crap ton of books that showed me the perils of being a magical being. I could wind up casting a spell that puts my head on my butt or worse killing someone. But as a human, the only hazards I faced were the normal kind. Okay, not so many differences but still, at least I wouldn't accidentally blow up the house because I couldn't handle my emotions.

There was also the question of Callie. By my mother's warnings, I pretty much would have to give up my best friend to enter this world of magic. That wasn't something I could ever imagine. Callie had been there for me from the beginning giving her up for the possibility to pull rabbits out of hats seemed like a selfish move.

But magic...

But Callie...

Ugh, my head hurts.

"Even worse because Callie and I were supposed to share a dorm at Brown. So not only would I be leaving her, but I'd be leaving her with some stranger. I don't know if she will ever forgive me for that."

She took my hand in hers, patting it. "I'm sure she will. You wouldn't have been best friends for this long if you let something small like this break you up. You can still talk to her, just don't tell her about being a witch." My mom shrugged like it was no big deal.

"But it's not small. I'm leaving her to face Brown alone so I can go be Sabrina, the Teenage Witch."

My mom giggled. "Not really. There's no finger-wagging involved." She paused for a moment and then winked. "Well, not much."

That was something, I guess. It gave me hope that I could possibly have Callie and my magical heritage too. I mean it was doable. I've kept things from Callie before. She still didn't know that Leo Bartlins didn't break up with her because he was gay but because I caught him cheating on her and threatened to rip his balls off if he ever went near her again. Leo still runs the other way every time he sees me.

I smiled despite myself and then sighed. "So, say I did want to go. What would that entail? Would I have to click my magical shoes together to get there?"

Rolling her eyes, my mom stood up and went to the island. Opening a drawer, she pulled out an envelope and brought it over to me. "Here. This is the school. It's actually here in Georgia. So, you can drive there." She grinned.

The envelope she tossed in front of me was the one I'd seen the other day. Winchester Academy. The blue-green emblem with a scroll and owl still decorated the corner of the paper. I tore the envelope open and pulled out the brochure that most colleges sent. Opening it up, it looked like a normal college. A big stone building with the smiling faces of their students staring back at me. Quotes sat next to each smiling face.

"Winchester Academy helped me find my destiny," a female voice said aloud, startling me into dropping the paper. I stared down at the picture of the brown-haired female student next to the quote. Her grin grew, and she winked at me, making me gasp.

"It's true!"

My mom cocked her head to the side. "And you still doubted it after everything?"

I slumped in my seat. "No, not really, but a part of me thought it was some elaborate dream, and I'd wake up any second."

"Well, it's not. I can promise you that." She grabbed the brochure and opened it up to another page. Pointing at the page, she said, "Here's the class list. Just like any other college, you want to focus on one course of study. Your first year, of course, can be spent finding out what exactly it is you're good at."

I glanced down at the paper and started to scan the course list. *Spellcasting 101. The Hazards of Potion Making. Herbology and Me.* On and on the list went. Some were classes that made sense to me, but others like the Black Arts creeped me out.

"Don't worry about picking anything right now." My mom placed her hand on top of mine. "You'll want to take the basics your first semester. Most of the kids going there will have a large advantage over you because they have been studying most of their lives. So, you'll need to play catchup."

"And whose fault is that?" I stuck my tongue out at her playfully.

"Hey, you'll thank me for it someday. Being a witch isn't all it's cracked up to be." My mom lifted her coffee mug up and gestured it toward me.

"Yeah, 'cause I'm sure being able to make money appear out of thin air is such a hardship," I said sarcastically, flipping through the brochure.

"About that." My mom stood up and took her cup to the sink. "That touches on some of those rules I was telling you about."

"What? I can't make money magically appear?" I gasped as if I hadn't already figured that out. "There goes my plans for world domination."

"Now, I didn't say that." My mom grinned, picking up her purse and putting it over her shoulder.

"Where are you going?" I raised a brow at her.

"We are going shopping for school supplies." She grinned, wiggling her car keys at me.

I frowned and rushed after her. "School supplies? You can get those here?"

"If you know where to look," my mom said mysteriously as she got into the car. We rode down the street, the music blaring and singing along to it as we headed toward wherever mom thought we could do school shopping.

What exactly did you buy for a witch school? A cauldron. Maybe a set of feathered quills. Or maybe I needed a familiar. I had allergies so I couldn't get a cat. Maybe a frog? People used frogs, right?

"What's running through your head?" my mom asked as we pulled into a normal looking strip mall.

Frowning at our surroundings, I said, "Just wondering what kind of shopping we would do. Like do I need a wand? Spellbooks?"

"A wand, no. But spellbooks, yes. You'll need quite a few." Mom led us toward the shopping strip and into a boring-looking knickknack store.

My nose wrinkled instantly at the incense filling the air. Walking down a line of shelves, holding glass cats and unicorn figurines, I asked, "Why are we here?"

"Patience." Mom's voice came from far away, and I turned to find her no longer near me. "Hurry up now, Maxine. We don't want to get separated."

I hurried toward her voice, catching glimpses of her blonde hair as I go around a corner. I moved further into the store a lot further than I expected it to go until the bookshelves started to be filled with other things, things that looked more like it should be in a Halloween shop than a knick-knack store. Crystal balls and jars filled with gelatin-like fluid and animal parts decorated the shelves with little price tags. Rows and rows of books changed the nose-tickling incense to a musty scent. My mouth dropped open, and I gaped around me. Who knew a store like this was sitting here and I never knew about it?

"Strange, isn't it?" My mom's voice popped up next to me, and I jumped, grabbing my chest.

"Don't do that!" I smacked her on the arm as she laughed. "How long has this been here?"

Mom glanced around the shop, thinking about it. "I'm not sure. Since I was a little girl. Most students of the Academy come here to replenish their supplies since it's so close to the school. Come on, over here." She grabbed my arm and led me to a shelf of bowls.

"Mom, I don't think I need kitchen supplies. I'm sure the school will have a cafeteria." I raised a brow and smirked.

She ignored my poke and grabbed a stone bowl from the shelf, bypassing the cedar ones next to it. "This is for crushing herbs for potions, not cooking." She picked up a weird little bat thing and handed it and the bowl to me. "You'll need these for your Potions 101 class. Also, you'll need ..." She reached out and grabbed a set of goggles that I actually recognized. We used the same kind for Chemistry.

49

I took the goggles and the bowl and bat thing in one arm as my mom started to put more things in my hands that I couldn't even begin to name. Struggling to hold on to all of them, I didn't see that part of the carpet was loose, but I sure figured it out when my foot found it.

Flying forward, I tried to keep a hold of the items in my hands, but I couldn't grab them and keep myself from face planting. Eyes squinted shut, I braced myself for the impact. However, before I hit the ground an arm wrapped around my waist and pulled me flush against a hard, warm chest.

I took my time opening my eyes. My hands curled into the fabric of the shirt on the most remarkable chest I'd ever had the pleasure to be pressed again. Blinking up at the neck that was attached to that gorgeous chest, I followed it up to a sculpted jaw finely covered in dark bristle. A pair of kissable lips sat below a strong nose and piercing hazel eyes. I could stare into those eyes forever. They were a mixture of green and gold that twinkled with amusement, I could only assume caused by me. My fingers itched to dig into the dark hair curling at the bottom of his neck and around his ears and find out if it was as soft as it looked.

"Maxine!" my mom's voice snapped me out of my hormonally induced haze.

Glancing at those kissable lips, which had curved up into a devilish smirk, I shook my head and pushed away from my delectable savior. "Uh, mom. Sorry, I think we need a basket." I searched around for the stuff I'd lost in the fall but found them floating above our heads. "Your doing?" I peeked over at the glorious specimen beside me.

"You're welcome," a low graveling voice answered, the sound of it doing something visceral to my body. I forced back the shiver of delight and focused on my mom, who seemed all too amused by the situation.

"Well, thank you. Whoever you are." My mom grinned at him and then winked at me.

The guy next to me didn't answer my mom's obvious question and simply nodded. He shot another panty melting smirk my way before heading into the shelves without another word. My eyes followed after him, dipping down low to the jeans covering his tight backside.

"Maxine!" My mom bumped me on the arm with a grin. "At least pretend not to be staring."

I couldn't help the grin on my face as I giggled. "Mom, stop." I blushed and ducked my head.

"Seems you're already making friends, and you aren't even at the school yet." My mom bumped me once more and started down the aisle again.

"Yeah, seems so." I followed after her and added, "Callie is going to be so jealous. She thinks Rhode Island guys are way hotter than Georgia guys. When she finds out someone like that is right here in town? She will have a field day." As if knowing I was talking about her, my phone buzzed.

Callie: Where you at? Want to go shopping for our dorm? I want a waffle maker.

I laughed at her silliness but then frowned. I still had to tell Callie my decision. I couldn't begin to think of how I would break the news to her. She would be so heartbroken. Betrayed. Not to mention she's a huge drama queen and would take this to the nth level.

"Well," my mom continued, not realizing I'm having a crisis right behind her, "I'm sure she will find plenty of Rhode Island hotties to keep her occupied. Now, while I'm not opposed to having a bit of fun, I do want you to make sure you're focusing on your studies. No one wants a sloppy spell caster." She chuckled and pulled a few more things off the shelves. "Believe me, I know. Once I turned my roommate into a rabbit for a week because I was too distracted to pay attention during transfigurations."

I nodded my head like I understood what she was saying. "Sure. Sure. I gotcha. Not something I plan to do."

"But you really should think about what you're going to tell Callie. She's really the only person that will notice you're gone. I mean, besides your dad and me." My mom put a basket on the counter where a way-too-normal-looking lady checked us out.

"Cash or card?" the woman asked.

My mom handed her a credit card as normal as can be.

I gaped at her. "What, no gold doubloons?"

The woman behind the counter raised a brow at me, and my mom held back a laugh. "No, nothing that old school. Really, Maxine, you shouldn't believe everything you watch or read. The magical community is pretty up to date on modern technology. They don't even require you to write your essays on parchment anymore."

"Oh, really?"

"Yeah, you can bring your laptop and cell." My mom took the bags the lady handed her, not at all noticing my sarcasm. "I think we've got everything you need. If you come across something I missed, just let me know, and I'll get it."

"Is there a uniform?" I asked, following her out of the store and back to our car. "I mean, like do I need to wear robes or a plaid skirt?"

My mom's face sobered, and she said with a completely straight face. "No, we wear blue jumpsuits with pointed hats. You'll get your own when you arrive."

For half a millisecond, I believed her and then frowned. "Not funny, mom."

"What? You asked." My mom grinned, sliding behind the steering wheel. "You can wear whatever you want. Though I'd stay away from plaid skirts." I gave her a questioning look, and she added, "You know, fetishes."

"Oh God, mom," I whined as my face scrunched up in disgust. "I don't need to know what you and dad do in the bedroom."

"Your dad's more of a whips and handcuffs kind of guy than a school girl kind." She laughed as I groaned in pure agony.

Thankfully, my phone buzzed again, reminding me that I hadn't answered Callie's message. Suddenly, my parent's sex life wasn't at the top of my lists of things to forget about. Though, it was a close race. It was time to talk to Callie.

Chapter 4

I WAS A COWARD. That's the only explanation for why I didn't tell Callie at the beginning of the summer that I wouldn't join her at Brown. I waited until the week before we were supposed to leave for Brown and also the exact moment that I arrived at Winchester Academy to send her a text.

Me: Hey Callie. I hate to do this over a text, but I can't make it to Brown. My grandmother has fallen ill, and with my parents overseas it's up to me to take care of her. Hopefully, I'll see you next semester.

Okay, I was the worst friend in the world. I wasn't the flea of best friends. In fact, I didn't even deserve to be called a best friend. On top of beating myself up about texting her the news of not going to Brown with her, I had to lie to her. The grandmother I told her about lived in California, so I knew she couldn't check up on me, but still, it killed me.

"Everything okay there, Max?" my mom asked. Also, my parents weren't overseas yet. Dad was, but mom was waiting until I got settled into school before joining him in Cairo for his newest expedition.

"Yeah, fine." I tucked my phone into my pocket and climbed out of the car. Meeting my mom at the trunk, I began to unload my bags onto the curb. Winchester Academy looked bigger than in the pictures. More ominous too. That also could be because of the iron fence circling the premises with sharp pointy tops.

My mom placed her hand on my arm as I tried to grab the next bag. "Are you sure? You don't have to do this. We could go home. You could go to Brown, and you could have a normal human life."

I stared at her for a moment. Yes was on the tip of my tongue but I couldn't make myself say it. I shook my head. "No, I'm good. I want to do this."

Mom nodded. "Okay, if you're sure. But remember, you can always call me. I will come back right away and get you." She pulled me into her arms and hugged me. I placed my hands on her back and held her tight. Hearing my mom say that I could change my mind, that I could fail if I wanted to make everything easier.

I gave mom one final squeeze before letting her go. Stepping back before I told her to take me home, I smiled. "Thank you for everything. I can't wait to hear all about Cairo."

"Well, at least let me help you get your bags up to your room." My mom tried to grab one of my bags, but I stopped her with a tight smile.

"I got it, mom." I patted her on the shoulder. "Please don't make me cry."

Seeing my struggle, mom nodded her own chin tight and quivering. "Alright, honey. I'll call you later tonight?"

"Yeah, I'll talk to you then."

I watched as my mom climbed back into the car, shut the door, and drove away, not once looking back. I sighed heavily when she was out of my view, glancing back at my bags and groaning.

"Need a hand?"

I spun around at the question and came face to face with an Adonis. Seriously, were there any ugly guys at in the magical community? He had light brown hair and chocolate brown eyes, his lips curved up into a grin. His blue t-shirt was stretched across his broad shoulders and clung to his chest like a second skin. I forced myself to keep my eyes up and not scan the rest of him like a drooling fangirl.

I did look down enough to see his finger pointed toward my pile of bags before I nodded. "Uh, yeah. Yes. I would love some help. My mom, she ..." I trailed off, looking toward where my mom had driven away.

"I get it," the Adonis answered with a grin that had my knees weak. "It's always hard when you leave home for the first time."

My eyes widened, and I stumbled over myself. "How do you know this is the first time? I mean, I could just have a bad mom, all too ready to kick me out of her house."

The Adonis chuckled a sound that had my inside curl deliciously. "I highly doubt that. Your mom seemed to love you a lot from where I was standing."

My lips ticked up at his words. "You were watching me?"

Unlike the guys from my high school, he didn't even blush at being caught. He only lifted two of my bags like they were nothing (and I knew they weighed a ton) before gesturing with his head toward the school. "You're in the first year's wing, right?"

"Yeah." I nodded, grabbing my other two bags which were thankfully quite a bit lighter. I followed after him as he made his way through the crowd of students, most of who moved out of his way without having to be asked. The females however stopped and stared just as I had, making me feel a bit better about my reaction.

"So, where to?" he asked finally when we arrived at the end of the hall.

"Uh ..." I dropped one of the bags and dug through my pocket, searching for my room assignment. "It's one fifteen."

"Alright, one fifteen it is." The Adonis moved through the hallway like he owned the place until he stopped before a closed door. "Here we are. One fifteen."

I stopped next to him and stared up at the numbers. An awkward silence filled the space between us before I realized he was waiting for me to open the door. I tried the handle, but it was locked.

Confused, I looked down at my room assignment paper again, but it didn't have any instructions on getting a key.

"You have to say your name to open your room," the Adonis next to me whispered in my ear.

I jumped slightly and then giggled a bit more than I should have before tucking my hair behind my ear. "Oh, right." Leaning forward, so my mouth was close to the door, I said, "Maxine Norman." This time when I tried the door handle, it opened for me.

"Ladies first." The Adonis nodded toward the dark inside.

Stepping into the room, I reach beside the door and found a light switch. I half expected to have to light a candle or a fireplace to light the room. I was beyond ecstatic to find out my mom hadn't been wrong about the college being up to date on modern technology.

Two twin beds sat on either side of the room with nightstands and desks on their respective sides. It looked like an ordinary dorm room. And I was worried. I laughed inwardly at myself.

I sat my bags next to the bed on the right and turned to see the Adonis set the other two bags on my bed. I stood there with my hands in my pockets as silence fell over us once more.

"I'd tip you, but I don't have any cash," I said for some reason and inwardly smacked myself.

The Adonis threw his head back and laughed. "That's alright. Learning your name was payment enough. Maxine Norman." He smirked at me and started for the door.

"Max!" I called out, stopping him in his tracks. "My name is Max."

Grinning once more, he inclined his head. "Alright, Max. I'm Paul. See you around."

"Okay, see you," I called out as he disappeared around the corner leaving me alone in my room. Shaking my head to get rid of the need to chase after him, I turned to my room. So, this would be my home for the next nine months. Well, it wasn't home, but it could be with a few touches.

I spent the next hour or so unpacking my bags and getting myself settled. When I was done, I collapsed on my bed, closing my eye briefly. Turning my head to the side, I opened them to see the empty bed next to me.

My roommate still hadn't made an appearance. I wondered what kind of person she was. Would she be my new best friend? Or would be enemies at first sight?

Thinking about best friends made me pick up my phone, which I'd put on silent. I had about a dozen messages and calls, all of them from Callie. I should look at them. Callie was probably freaking out. Wondering what the hell I was thinking, no doubt.

Before I could look at them and ease her worries, there was a sound at the dorm room door. A muffled feminine voice muttered something unintelligible before the door opened.

A pretty, petite girl walked in, her dark hair a curly afro on her head topped with a cute blue headband. She wore a pair of blue jean shorts and a yellow tank top covered by a blue vest. She struggled to get her bags in behind her, cursing as one of the bags caught on the door frame.

"Here," I said, hurrying to the door to help her out. "Let me help."

The girl looked up and saw me, relief washed over her face. "Thanks."

I helped her bring her bags in from the hallway and sat them on the left side of the room. "I hope you don't mind. I took the right."

"No, no. That's totally fine." She tossed her bags onto her bed before turning and offering me her hand. "I'm Trina."

"Max." I smiled and shook her hand. "So, you're a first year too?"

Trina ducked her head. "Is it that obvious?"

I chuckled. "Well, we are in the first year's dorm. So, it was fairly obvious."

"Oh, right." Trina smacked herself on the forehead. "I swear I'm not this helpless. I'm just all ..." She waved her hands in front of her.

"Disoriented? Completely out of your element?" I grinned harder.

"Yeah. That."

"Me too." I tucked my hands in my back pockets. "Actually, until a few months ago, I didn't even know I was a witch."

"Really?" Trina's eyes widened. "How is that even possible?"

I shrugged. "A mother who wanted to marry a human and give me a normal life."

"Then how did you end up here? Shouldn't you be at a human college?" Trina asked. I could tell she sincerely wanted to know and wasn't being malicious at all.

"I was supposed to be at a human college. Brown actually." I sighed and moved back over to sit on my bed. "I didn't find out about my witchy heritage until my powers couldn't be contained by my mom's repressor spell."

"Wow, a brain and a badass. Color me impressed."

I chuckled. "Don't be. I thought I was a mutant or some kind of alien."

"How'd you find out?" Trina asked, leaning against her bed as well. "I mean, what triggered it?"

I shrugged. "A jack ass ex-boyfriend and nerves wound way too tight." I sighed and tugged on my hair. "Let's just say things were burned, and I almost checked myself into an insane asylum."

"That blows." Trina puffed out. "Well, I'm glad you figured it out and ended up here. I'd have hated to get a weirdo for a roommate."

"Well, I can promise that I'm not that." I paused and thought for a moment. "At least, I don't think so. So, what about you? How long have you known you were a witch?"

"Since forever really." Trina pounced on the bed a bit, her face scrunched together in concentration. "I mean, I'm sure there were a specific date and time, but I don't remember it. I was too young. But the moment I started showing signs of powers, my mom began teaching me. Then, like all the others, I went to Winchester Prep for grade school, and now I'm here."

"There's a Winchester Prep?" I arched a brow.

"Well, yeah. I mean, there are other schools for minor witches and wizards, but around here, most go there." Trina stood and clapped her hands on her thighs. "I'm starved. Want to find the cafeteria and then scope out the local hotties?"

Her mention of hotties made me think of Callie once more and my smile wilted. "Uh, yeah sure. Give me a second. I need to use the bathroom first."

"Sure," Trina said, and we both headed out of the room.

Trina waited at the door of the bathroom down the hall as I headed inside. I pulled my phone out of my pocket and took a deep breath before braving the hysteria that was probably Callie.

Not only were there a dozen or more messages most of them an array of 'what the hell''s and 'really? answer me''s. There were a few threats on my life that I didn't take too seriously, but the voicemail really got to me.

"Max, this is Callie. You know, your best friend and life partner? If you could even call me that anymore. I can't believe you are leaving me here to take on the Brown hotties all on my own. I understand families important, but you know, I'm important too." Her voice broke slightly, and I felt my eyes welling up. "I need my best friend here. I need you." She took a deep breath and let it out into the phone. "Please, Max. Just call me. Call me back."

I didn't call Callie back. I couldn't if I tried. I knew if I did, I'd break. I wouldn't be able to lie to her, and I'd be breaking one of the biggest rules of being a witch. I'd only just learned about it all I couldn't lose it already.

Shoving my phone back into my pocket, I washed my hands before heading out the door.

Trina looked up from her phone and smiled at me. "Ready?"

"Yeah, sure. Let's go." I'd smooth things over with Callie later when I was alone. I had to go into this head first and not think about my previous life even if it meant lying my butt off.

Chapter 5

WINCHESTER ACADEMY WAS A virtual maze. One minute, Trina and I were walking down the hallway toward the front of the building, and the next moment we were staring at a row of creepy doors with no one in sight.

"Maybe we should have grabbed the campus map?" Trina suggested, turning around in a circle.

"There's a map?"

"Oh, yeah. In the welcome packet. Didn't you get one?" Trina frowned, her brows furrowed. "It had a map, our class schedule, where to get your I.D., and everything." I just looked at her with even more confused. "You really didn't get one?"

I had no clue what she was talking about. If I had gotten a welcome packet, my mom would have said so. I certainly would have memorized every word of it before coming. Overachiever right here. The fact that I was missing it did not bode well for the start of my college career.

"No, I didn't. I thought I'd get all that when I arrived," I explained, placing my hands on my hips with a sigh.

"Well, you'll have to go to the administration office to get it then ... if we can find the place." She searched around us once more, trying to figure out which way we should go.

After a few moments of nothing changing, I dug into my pocket and pulled out a quarter. "Maybe we should flip for it? Heads, we go straight, tails, we try and go back the way we came?" I glanced at Trina for confirmation. She nodded, and I flipped the coin in the air. We watched it fly up, turning over and over and I prepared to catch it, but then suddenly it flew out of the air and straight into the hallway where it landed in the hand of a beautiful girl.

"Lost, are we?" the girl said, closing her hand over the quarter and grinned.

"Uh, yeah." I cocked my head to the side as I assessed the blonde girl who was flanked by two others female students.

"Not surprised," she said with a flip of her long silky blonde hair. The beautiful girl strutted down the hallway in a pair of pink high heels. Her pleated black skirt swayed with her every movement. If I'd been into girls, I'd have definitely been drooling. However, since I was more into the male of the species, I could only look at her with stars in my eyes.

The two girls by the blonde's side followed as if they were of one mind. One was also a blonde with a chest so large I wondered how she stayed upright, her blue eyes vacant and empty of emotion. The other one had brown hair that fell in waves down her back with a kind of half smile on her lips. They each wore their own version of the first girl's outfit, complete with pleated skirts and high heels.

Jerking my attention back to the first girl who had started talking again, I pretended I wasn't developing a girl crush.

"It's just like you nobodies to end up where you don't belong," she said with a disgusted tone. She waved a finger in the air around us. "This area is for people who matter, and that doesn't include you." She held out her hand with the coin, and I reached for it, but she dropped it before I could take it. The coin landed on the ground with a clink. "Oops, sorry," she crooned, not at all sincere.

"Oh, it's fine," Trina quickly said, bending down to pick up the coin, her voice a higher pitch than before. "We're sorry. Didn't mean to overstep our bounds." She grabbed my arm and started to pull me in the opposite direction. "Come on, Max."

"Actually," - I removed my arm from her grasp - "I think I like it right here."

Trina stopped trying to grab at me and went silent.

The main blonde girl's eyes narrowed a warning smile on her lips. "Oh, is that so? Maybe I'm mistaken."

Her friends gasped, and the brunette shook her head. "There's no way. You're never wrong. They're bottom feeders. I can smell it."

The big boobed blonde leaned forward and sniffed the air. "Yeah, smells like ... tacos."

The blonde leader rolled her eyes at her friends and then focused back on me. "Where are my manners? I forgot the introductions. I'm Sabrina Craftsman." She flipped her hair and grinned like her name was supposed to mean something.

The way that Trina stiffened beside me told me it should have, but it didn't to me, which meant she was just another girl who thought she was too hot for common manners.

Apparently, I didn't respond the way she wanted me to because Sabrina continued. "You know Craftsman Spellwork? My father is Xander Craftsman. He revolutionized the way we work spells." She kept going as I stared at her blankly. "What is wrong with you? You should be kissing my feet right now."

I shrugged. "Sorry, never heard of you."

Her cronies giggled, but when Sabrina shot a glare back at them, they quickly shut up. Turning back to me, Sabrina snarled, "And who are you?"

Grinning from ear to ear, I held my hand out. "Max. Nice to meet you."

Sabrina stared down at my hand like I had just handed her a bag of trash. "Max what?"

I frowned and then glanced back at Trina. "What do you mean?"

Stomping her foot like a petulant child, Sabrina snapped, "Max what? Who are your people? Where do you stand in the magical community?"

I chuckled lightly. "Oh. Norman. My last name's Norman and as far as where I stand in the magical community ..." I glanced around the hallway. "Well, for the moment I stand right here with you all."

The brunette clearly was trying to hide a laugh and covered it up by pretending to cough. The other blonde didn't seem to get my joke. Someone was missing a few crayons in their box.

Sabrina, however, clearly understood me. Stepping into my personal space, she moved in until our nose almost brushed. "You think you are so funny, don't you? Well, let me tell you something, Norman. The people at this school respect my family and me. They would do anything to be friends with me, meaning they would do anything for me. And people like you?" She flicked my shoulder, and I raised my brows at her ridiculousness. "You're big nobodies, just in the way of the real talent. So, get comfortable with that thought, it'll make things a lot easier for you. Are we clear?"

I forced back a grin and nodded. "Oh, we're clear."

"Good." Sabrina moved back and smiled smugly. Turning to her friends, she clicked her fingers. "Come on, I'm hungry."

Before she could get too far away, I cleared my throat. "There *is* one thing I'm not so clear on that maybe you could clear up for me?"

Sabrina froze in her steps but didn't turn around. "What's that?"

Brows furrowed, I tapped my chin in thought. "Do your parents hate you or did they just really love nineties sitcoms, because I have to tell you, naming your witch child Sabrina?" I chuckled again. "Really not fair."

Sabrina's shoulders shook, and her fingers curled into fists, her friends watching in awe and horror. For a second, I thought Sabrina was going to turn me into a toad for daring to make fun of her name, but she simply straightened her back, let out a ragged breath, and kept walking.

When they were well out of eyeshot, Trina smacked me on the shoulder. "Holy shit, Max. You have balls. I could never have done something like that, especially to a Craftsman."

I smiled down at her. "I don't like bullies, and people like Sabrina only have power because people give it to her."

"Well, she does have a point." Trina continued as we followed the way the trio had gone. "People do respect and fear her family. She could have the whole school against you for what you said."

"She's that petty, huh?"

"You wouldn't believe it." Trina snorted and puffed her hair. "That girls got deep-seated problems starting from the silver spoon her parents shoved up her ass."

When we finally found our way out of the hallway and into the main quad, I let out a sigh. Here they at least had signs.

"There's the cafeteria." I pointed at the sign directing us to the left where the smell of something delicious wafted toward us.

"And there's the administration office." Trina nodded to the left. "You should probably head there. No doubt the line will be long, and you don't want to end up missing your first day of classes."

I glanced between the cafeteria and the administration office. My stomach grumbled its opinion of where I should go, but I knew Trina was right. If I didn't get my class schedule, I'd have to spend tomorrow playing catch up. Frowning at being a grown-up, I turned toward the left.

"Want me to bring you something back?" Trina asked as I started to walk toward the office.

I glanced over my shoulder. "Yeah, just grab me a sandwich or something. That'd be great."

"You got it." Trina clicked her fingers and skipped toward the cafeteria.

Chuckling at my roommate, I didn't see the person coming out of the administration office until it was too late. My head turned, and my nose smashed into the walking wall of beef. Crying out, I grabbed my nose, rubbing it for good measure as I glared up at the perpetrator.

74

"Watch where you're going!" I swallowed my words as my mouth went dry and all my irritation vanished, replaced by trepidation. The chest I had slammed into belonged to a very large, very frightening looking guy who cocked a brow at me.

"Yes?" The deep voice belonging to the mountain before me wasn't quite as scary as how he looked but had a smooth undertone that did ridiculous things to my insides. What the hell was wrong with me? This guy could give a professional wrestler a run for his money, and here I was, drooling over him.

"I ... I mean, uh." I chuckled nervously. "Excuse me. I'm new here and a bit on edge."

The guy tilted his head to the side, the edge of his lips twitching as if he wanted to smile but refused to.

Not sure what else to do, I inclined my head and pointed toward the office letting another nervous laugh. "I've gotta go in there. Yeah, bye."

Darting around him, I pushed the office door open only to see a line so long I'd be missing lunch and dinner. Groaning in dismay, I checked my phone. More messages from Callie waited on the screen. I couldn't very well call her out here in the open, but I couldn't make her wait any longer. After all, I had time to spare.

Me: Hey Callie, sorry for the late response. I couldn't answer my phone on the plane.

Callie's answer was immediate, and it made my throat tighten. She had been waiting for my message. Probably spent all day just biting her nails.

Callie: Where the hell have you been? I'm calling you!

My phone started to ring as I tried to text her not to. I got a series of glares from the others in line, and I quickly hit ignore. Taking a deep breath in, I got ready to lie my ass off.

Me: Sorry again. I can't talk right now. My grandma has a lot of people over to check on her.

Callie: Then at least explain to me wtf is going on?

Me: I told you. I have to take care of my grandma until my parents get back from Cairo.

Callie: But what about Brown? All our plans!

Me: I know. I'm sorry. There's nothing I can do.

A throat cleared behind me and I looked up from my phone to see the line had moved and I hadn't. Shooting an apologetic look to the person behind me, I moved further up in the line before looking at my phone again.

Callie: I know, but it still doesn't suck any less. What am I going to do with all the hotties here by myself?

I giggled. Callie never could stop thinking with her hormones. I shifted up the line once more before texting Callie once more.

Me: I'm sure you'll do fine without me. ;)

Callie: Well call me when you can. Miss you already! <3

Tucking my phone back into my pocket, I sighed. That wasn't as bad as I expected. Not that I believed for one second that Callie was going to let me off the handle this easily. I expected a long and drawn out conversation was due in the near future, right after I got myself squared away.

"Next!" a slightly irritated voice shouted out, and I glanced around the long line to catch a glimpse of a messy mop of reddish brown hair and a shuffling of papers. Those same papers flew through the air and toward a pile by the door, stacking into a neat pile. I gaped at the first sign of magic I'd seen since getting to Winchester Academy.

"I wish I still had that kind of wonderment just from a small flotation spell." I spun around to see the same dark head of hair that had saved me from face planting at the knick-knack store.

"You!" I gaped, pointing a finger at him, earning me an amused smirk. "I mean, again. I mean ..." I dragged a hand over my hair. "You go here too?" The guy standing between us gave us both curious looks but just watched.

The black-haired beauty chuckled. "Yes, I do. Have been for two years now." He gestured his head toward the line. "You should probably move up. It's almost your turn, and you don't want Dale pissed off at you."

I turned around toward the line where the reddish-brown head was coming closer into view. This Dale guy must be a real piece of work if tall, dark, and handsome was worried about him. Glancing back at him, I told my heart to stop fluttering when he winked at me.

"Next!"

My smile deepened as the dark-haired beauty continued to smirk at me. I forgot about the other people in the room, the fact that I was in line, or even that my best friend in my back pocket was waiting for me to call her. There was nothing but me and those gold sparkles in his eyes.

"Next!" I only had a half second to process the words before I was bombarded with a dozen paper airplanes. Covering my head with my hands, I tried to swat away the planes, but they just kept coming. Eventually, when I was curled into a ball on the ground, they stopped.

I slowly dropped my arms and peeked my eyes open to see everyone staring at me. Even the dark-haired beauty had stopped to see the show. I uncurled from the ground and scrambled to my feet, adjusting my clothes and hair as I went.

"Now, if you're done using my waiting area to make moon eyes at Broomstein, can you tell me what you want so we can all get on with our lives?" a voice full of barely contained sarcasm asked me and my face flushed as I turned around.

While I was making moon eyes as I'd been accused of, the line had moved, and it was now my turn. The reddish-brown head belonged to an attractive intellectual man. He even had glasses and a pocket protector. Blushing even more, I moved to the edge of the desk.

"Sorry, I—"

"Save the excuses. Name?" The guy held a tablet in front of him, his stylus poised and ready to find me.

"Maxine Norman," I stuttered out, twisting my hands in front of me as he scrolled through the tablet until he pointed at a name on the list.

"What do you need?" his voice had a no-nonsense tone that made me hesitant to tell him how royally screwed I was.

"Uh, I ..."

"Come on, I don't have all day. Others are waiting to waste my time." He gestured his stylus toward the line behind me.

"Right, I'm sorry," I started but paused when a dark shadow filled my peripherals.

Dark-haired beauty had cut in line to stand beside me. Dale's eyes moved from me to him, and he pointed his stylus at him. "Wait your turn, Broomstein. I'll get to you."

"Knock it off, Dale," Broomstein said, tapping his knuckles on the counter. "I don't know who spit in your coffee this morning but stop taking it out on the first years. Can't you see she's a bit overwhelmed?"

I started to argue my case, but both guys continued as if I weren't standing right there.

"Go find someone else to pester, Ian. I'm busy." Dale bit out, finally giving me my savior's name. Ian. It suited him.

"Go ahead, Max." Ian grinned at me. "Tell Dale what you need. He'll get you fixed up and then hopefully pull that broomstick out of his ass."

I stifled a giggle when Dale glared. "I didn't get my welcome packet."

Dale frowned at my admission. "That's strange. Every student should have received one. I sent them out myself."

I shrugged. "Well, there must have been a mistake because I didn't get one."

The sharpness of the look Dale gave me made me wince. "I don't make mistakes." He glanced back down at his tablet, and his frown deepened. "Do you have your room assignment?"

Reaching into my back pocket, I pulled out the paper I'd received in the mail with my acceptance letter. "Yeah, I already put my stuff away though."

He snatched the paper from my hands and found my student number at the top of the page. Typing into his little tablet, he scowled. "There are two students under this number. A Maxine Norman and a Maxine Mancaster. Which one are you?"

Chapter 6

A PEN COULD DROP, and everyone could hear it with how silent the office became. Not sure what the fuss was about, I glanced around curiously and then back to Dale.

"Uh, I guess both." I flushed and ducked my head before peeking up at Ian. He smiled at me as if this was all an everyday occurrence for him.

Dale, however, wasn't happy with my answer. "Either you are, or you're not. You can't be both."

Sighing, I threw my hands up. "Yes, I can actually. My dad's last name is Norman. That's what it says on my birth certificate and my I.D. which I've stupidly left back in my room." I kept going before Dale could start arguing with me once more. "My mom's maiden name is Mancaster. I don't know why I'm in the system twice. I only sent in information for the first name."

There were a few gasps and whispering behind me, but I ignored them and waited for Dale to figure out what happened.

Dale let out an aggravated grunt. "Well, someone put you in twice, but now it makes sense why you wouldn't get a welcome packet."

"It does?" I asked, not understanding his thought process.

He clicked a few things on his tablet and then picked up the phone next to him. After dialing some numbers, he said into the phone, "Yes, sir? That Mancaster girl is here." A pause as whoever was on the other end answered. "Yes. I'll send her right in."

Pursing my lips together, I frowned harder. "I'm sorry. Maybe it's because I'm so new to this whole magic stuff," - Ian snorted at my mention of magic stuff - "but can you tell me what is going on? Am I in some kind of trouble?"

Shaking his head so that his hair fell over the brim of his glasses, Dale sighed as if answering me was so much more work than it actually was. "No, you're not in trouble. The Headmaster likes to greet students that come from certain families before they start school. Not sending you a welcome packet makes it so that you have to come by." He said it in a way that made me think that talking to the Headmaster wasn't exactly a pleasant encounter.

"Oh, okay." I paused and then pointed behind him. "So, I talk to the Headmaster, and then I can get my schedule and everything?"

"Yes, yes. He's back there." Dale gestured a thumb behind him and then looked at Ian. "What do you want?"

Ian lifted his hands in front of him and grinned. "Nothing, I'm good."

"Then why are you here?" Dale growled, waving a hand to make him move out of the line.

I watched Ian shifted away from the line, curious about what exactly he was doing in the office if he didn't need anything. Shooting me one of his devilish smirks, Ian headed for the door. "Good to see you again, Max."

A bit flushed, all my brain cells heading directing between my thighs, I completely forgot I was supposed to be seeing the Headmaster until another paper airplane hit me in the back of the head.

I narrowed my eyes at Dale as I rounded the counter toward the door he had pointed at before. Dale didn't even acknowledge me, his focus fully on his next victim.

When I stopped before the door marked 'Headmaster,' my nerves decided to kick back in. That pesky ball of light inside of me started to prickle at the back of my eyes, and I could feel my fingertips buzzing. I thought back to my mom's last words of advice to me before we left for school.

"Just breathe. The worst thing you could do when you feel like you're about to lose control is to forget to breathe. In through your nose, and out through your mouth."

I breathed deep through my nose and held it for a moment. Before I could let it out, another paper airplane smacked me in the back of the head, making me let out my breath in a rush. Annoyance replaced nervousness, and I used that to quickly knock on the door in front of me.

A voice from inside beckoned me inside. I didn't have a chance to turn the knob before the door opened for me. A little bit creeped out and my nerves threatening to come back up, I stepped into the large office.

A large leatherback chair sat behind a mahogany brown desk. The older man in the chair wasn't the thing that surprised me. He seemed like he could be one of my grandfather's best friends from the golf club with his short white beard and rosy cheeks, and the suit he wore looked like it cost at least a couple of thousand dollars. No, the thing that surprised me was the desktop with dual monitors and a processor big enough to handle any video game the player could throw at it.

"Miss Mancaster." The headmaster stood from his desk and rounded it to stand before me. He offered me an aged hand, and I shook it with a polite smile.

"Uh, headmaster." I nodded. "And it's actually Norman, not Mancaster."

The headmaster's smile wilted slightly but didn't disappear completely. "Of course, I had forgotten your mother had insisted on taking her human husband's last name." I chose to ignore the little bit of indignation that filled the headmaster's voice as he spoke about my dad. It seemed that not everyone had the same respect for humans. It didn't bode well for my chances of fitting in.

"I don't mean to be rude, headmaster ...?"

"Swordson."

"Headmaster Swordson." I nodded to make sure I had it right. "But I don't understand why I'm here?"

"Why you're here at this school?" Headmaster Swordson cocked his head to the side. "I would think that was fairly obvious. I'm sure your mother explained to you what kind of school this is?"

I shook my hands in front of me. "No, I don't mean here as in the school. I mean, here in your office. Dale said I had to meet you to get my class schedule and the rest of my welcome packet?" I smacked my lips together and rocked on my heels. "Well, it looks like we met, so can I have my stuff now?" I knew I sounded kind of rude, but the headmaster hadn't really been all that welcoming to me, and the longer I stood in his office, the more I felt like he wasn't going to be my biggest fan.

"My, my, you are your mother's daughter." Headmaster Swordson chuckled lightly, shaking his head.

"Excuse me?"

"Your mother had quite the head on her shoulders as well. Never was one for political bullshit." I gaped at the headmaster. Maybe I had assessed him a bit too soon. "Forgive me, my dear, but after doing this job for two decades, your failure to fall at my feet with promises of blessings from your family makes you a breath of fresh air."

Completely confused but for some reason feeling a bit better about the whole situation, I decided to start again. "I think we've got off on the wrong foot."

"I think so too. Let's start over." The headmaster leaned against the front of his desk and crossed one leg over the other, his hands splayed on the desk behind him. "My name is Oliver Swordson, I am the headmaster of this school. It is my job to make sure that the young men and women of the magical community have the proper direction to what kind of career they will pursue. Whether that be in the short term or the long term. Another part of my job is to make sure that certain members of certain prestigious families are ..." He trailed off and waved a hand in front of him. "... well taken care of."

I thought I was starting to understand what he was getting at, but it didn't make sense why I was in his office. Then it clicked. "So, you're saying I'm from one of those prestigious families?" I pointed a finger at myself with a half laugh. "Me? Maxine Norman?"

The headmaster shook his head with a small smile. "Not Maxine Norman. Maxine Mancaster. Your mother might have given up her name when she married your human father, but that doesn't mean that the Mancaster blood doesn't still run through your veins."

"And the Mancasters are a big deal?" I squinted at him like it would make what he was saying anymore clearer.

"Oh, quite a big deal. Your grandparents are quite the philanthropists. They have their hands in quite a few areas of interest." He chuckled again as if it were the funniest thing he had ever heard.

I shook my head. "I didn't know. My grandparents aren't exactly in touch ... well ... ever."

The headmaster stopped chuckling and sobered. "Completely understandable. Your mother marrying a human, while isn't unheard of in our community, it was seen as a slap in the face to some magical families."

What he wasn't saying was that my mom did something her parents - my grandparents - didn't approve of and they gave her the boot in return. I'd heard of parents not agreeing with some of their kids' decisions, but really disowning someone and then cutting ties with them completely because you didn't like your daughter's choice in spouses? That was a bit far.

"Okay, so my grandparents are loaded and spend a lot of money. What does that mean for me? Because as far as I'm concerned, they didn't want to be a part of my life. Why should I care about them?" I crossed my arms over my chest and frowned.

Nodding slightly, the headmaster tapped his fingers on the desk. "I understand your trepidation to get involved with your mother's family after the way they left things, but you don't need to be involved with them to be able to reap the benefits of your name."

"And what would that entail?" I inched forward in my seat, leaning forward on my arms.

"Well ..." The headmaster moved to sit behind his desk. "That depends on you. If you assume your mother's maiden name, your family name, then you would get all the perks that name provides, but you will also be expected to act like someone of the Mancaster family."

I frowned at his explanation. Perks were always a plus. I could use those at a school where I was already the new kid as well as years behind the rest, but something told me the cost for those perks might be more than I wanted to pay.

"Thank you, Headmaster." I stood to my feet. "You have given me a lot to think about. I'm not sure I will be taking my grandparent's name just yet, but it's good to know I have the option." I nodded and turned to head toward the door.

"Miss Norman?"

I paused at the headmaster's voice and turned back. "Yes?"

"You can get your welcome packet with your class schedule from Mr. Varns up front. He will also be in charge of giving you a tour of the campus." I smiled and nodded again, but the headmaster wasn't done. "And Miss Norman, welcome to Winchester Academy. I have a feeling this will be an interesting year."

Smiling at the older man, I ducked out of his office before he could keep me longer. Back in the reception area, I found the same line as before though considerably shorter. Mr. Varns, which I could only assume was Dale, still stood behind the desk snapping at students as they passed through his line.

I walked up next to him with a slight smirk.

"What do you want?" Dale growled and then snapped his fingers at the next student in line.

"Headmaster Swordson told me to get my welcome packet and class schedule from you." I shifted from foot to foot waiting for Dale to explode with the irritation which seemed to be his go-to reaction to everything and everyone.

Instead of an aggravated grunt or attacking me with another paper airplane, he stopped helping the student in front of him and opened his desk drawer. Flipping through a file, he grabbed a packet of papers and then shoved them into my arms.

I glanced down at the packet. A map of the campus sat on top and beneath it was my class schedule, the student handbook, as well as my sign in for the school computer system. Clutching the papers to my chest, I looked back at Dale who had dismissed me completely.

"What could you possibly want now?" he groaned as he turned away from the student in front of him to glare at me. "You have your packet. You can leave."

A sly grin slid over my lips. "Actually, I don't have everything I need. Headmaster Swordson said I'm entitled to a tour."

"Okay, fine. I'll get one of the second years over here in a minute." He tried to turn away from me, but I tapped him on the shoulder.

"Actually," I drew out and clicked my tongue, "Headmaster Swordson wants you to give it to me." I braced myself for an attack of paper airplanes, holding my packet of papers as a shield over my face. Thankfully, it never came. Nor did anything else. The room went silent. Moving the papers away from my face slowly, I found the entire line of students frozen in place.

I turned to Dale and gaped as he put his tablet down and grabbed his cell phone and a black messenger bag as if everything were fine. He glanced up at me as he rounded the desk. "Are you coming?"

"Wait, what?" I pointed at the line of frozen students as I followed after him. "What about them? You can't just leave them like that."

"Sure, I can." Dale adjusted his glasses on his nose. "They won't even know we were gone. Well, if we get going. The spell doesn't last that long, and if you are going to ask this many questions before the tour has even started, then it'll wear off before we get back." He gave me one more impatient look before starting into the quad not looking back to see if I was following.

Welcome to Winchester Academy, indeed.

Chapter 7

DALE STARTED RIGHT OFF into the quad and started spouting off facts about the campus before I could even catch up to him.

"Over there is the cafeteria." He pointed a finger toward where Trina had gone. "It's open eight to eight. If you don't make it by closing time, you're tough out of luck. There are a few places that deliver here, but most students choose to save their money for more important things." He ran his eyes over me, pure indignation clear on his face. "Something I'm sure you don't worry about," he said matter-of-factly before turning away, not giving me a chance to ask what the heck that meant.

He moved to the hallway I recognized as the one we had come out of. "That's where the students of the more privileged families stay, though I'm sure you know that already," he said with the same kind of disdain as before.

"Why would you assume that?" I did know where the hallway led because of my encounter with Sabrina and her squad, but he didn't know that. I was also getting tired of his tone as if I was an annoying bug buzzing around his ear.

Dale paused for a moment and frowned. "You're a Mancaster. Of course, you're staying in the privileged hallway."

"No, I'm not." I shook my head, my eyes wide. "I'm with the rest of the first years."

Brow furrowed in confusion, Dale held out his hand. "That's not right. Let me see your room assignment."

I handed him the paper like before, and he squinted at the paper as if his eyes weren't working. Unsatisfied, he shoved the paper back at me and turned on his heel. "Must have been a mix-up. I'm sure the headmaster can straighten it out."

Hurrying after him, I put the paper away with the packet in my hands. "But what if I don't want to fix it? What if I like it right where I am?"

Dale stopped again without warning, and I slammed into his back, causing my packet of papers to fly everywhere. Dropping to my knees, I scurried to pick up the papers before they got trampled on by the other students.

Dale just stared down at me as if seeing me for the first time.

When one of the papers ended up on the other side of the hallway, Dale sighed. The paper zipped toward me, and I had a heartbeat of a second to duck before it landed on the pile in my hands. Climbing back to my feet, I muttered, "Thanks."

"Why wouldn't you want to stay with the privileged families?" Dale asked suspiciously, his arms crossed over his chest. "It's where you belong."

I shrugged. "Says who?"

"You're a Mancaster," he insisted.

"So? That's my grandparent's name, not mine. I'm a Norman, and I'm perfectly happy in the first year's dorms." I stared him down, daring him to question me.

After a moment or two, Dale clicked his tongue and shook his head before starting down a different hallway. I had a feeling he didn't like my answer. Or maybe I'd confused his know-it-all sensibilities? Either way, I wasn't making friends with Dale any time soon.

"Down this hall will be the majority of your classes for most majors." He quirked his fingers, and my schedule slipped out of my pile and into his hands. His eyes scanned it behind his glasses, and if possible, his eyes narrowed even further. "You're taking all remedial courses?"

Not sure if it was really a question, I said, "Uh, yeah. Thought it best if I started with the basics."

Dale turned almost running me over and held the paper out between us, shaking it slightly as he talked. "Don't you know any magic?"

I shook my head. "Nope."

"None at all?"

Sighing, I shifted the packet of papers in my hands again. "Well, I didn't know I was a witch until a few months ago, and my mom was more focused on making sure I didn't blow up the house than showing me how to freeze an entire room. How did you do that again?"

"It's a third-year spell," was his simple answer before continuing his interrogation. "How is it that you have no knowledge of magic and still standing here?"

Lifting a shoulder and then dropping it, I really had no idea. I'd gotten the letter in the mail and just assumed everyone got one. I hadn't even had to take a test or anything to get in.

After a moment of studying me, Dale seemed to come to a conclusion, one that didn't make him happier to be with me.

"Well, you might not go by the name, but you're a Mancaster through and through. Already getting by with minimal effort." He snorted and shoved the paper back into my hands.

My eyes trailed after him for a moment, my mouth gaping open at him. When he barked at me to hurry up, I clamped my mouth closed and jogged after him.

"You're wrong, you know," I told him after a few moments of silence. "I'm not getting by on my name alone."

"Oh, really?" Dale sniffed. "That would be a surprise."

"Really," I told him with all certainty. "My mom married a human. My grandparents probably don't even know my name or that I exist. Or at least they pretend not to. I've never met them."

Dale's expression seemed to soften a bit but still no smile. "Well, I know all about uncaring families. My own didn't want me to go to college."

"Oh? What'd they want you to do?" I asked, genuinely curious about what made him tick. There had to be a reason he hated the privileged so much. I mean besides the obvious.

Dale tucked his hands into his pockets and kept his eyes forward. "My dad works for the Order of Merlin." When I just stared blankly at him, he added, "That's what we magical folks call our government. He's a paper pusher, but he didn't go to college for a specialty. He expected me to do the same as him as well as my three brothers."

"Wow, you have three brothers?" I asked, a bit dazzled by all the new information. "I'd love to have siblings. I'm an only child which is great sometimes, you know no sharing, but other times, not so much. It can get kind of lonely. I guess that's why I always made sure to find friends I could talk to."

Green eyes studied me before Dale said, "You won't find a lack of friends here. If you know where to look that is." We stopped before a set of double doors. "You also have to watch out for those who would want to use you for your name."

I nodded. "Yeah, I got that much from the headmaster which is why I'm not going by Mancaster." I chewed on my lower lip for a moment and then added, "So, if you could keep that between us, I'd appreciate it."

"You won't hear it from me, but there were a dozen students in the office that won't give you the courtesy," Dale reminded me with a serious look. "I can do a slight memory spell if you really want to stay out of the limelight."

"Really? That would be great!" I grinned up at him.

Dale shrugged. "It won't make them forget it completely, but it'll make things blurry enough they won't pay you any mind." He shifted uncomfortably. "It's not full proof, so I would be prepared for it to come out."

"Gotcha." I turned toward the doors and asked, "So, what's in here? The broomstick closet?"

For the first time, I got a smile out of Dale. It was small, but it was a start. With one hand on the door, he pushed it open slowly. "This is my favorite part of the campus. The library."

Every definition of the word library was completely and utterly wrong when applies to this place. The opera house-sized room Dale led me into wasn't just a library, it was a sanctuary for books and knowledge seekers alike.

Three stories of bookshelves stuffed with books filled the majority of the floor plan. Large columns held up the other floors with stairs leading to each level. Set sporadically throughout the shelves were tables only big enough for four people, but what the room lacked for in group space, it made up for in individual comfy chairs in every nook and cranny.

Dale led me into the heart of the library, his eyes sparkling with excitement. "As you can tell, they discourage large groups in here."

"Why's that?" I murmured, suddenly not wanting to talk too loudly lest I disturb the books.

"The school believes it will lower the likelihood of people messing around when they should be studying. It's a library after all." Dale placed a hand on his hip and pushed up his glasses with one finger. A burst of laughter and chatter interrupted the quiet solace of the library making Dale's eyes narrow. "But despite the school's efforts, some mischief makers always seem to slip through the cracks." He nodded toward the group of six who shoved in around one of the small tables.

I started to smile at their obvious disregard for the rules until I noticed a certain blonde poufy head. Sabrina turned and smiled at the attractive male squeezed in next to her at the table, her friends in similar positions with their own guys.

Unable to let out the groan, I tried to back out of the library without being seen. Unfortunately, backing out meant I didn't see the chair behind me until it was too late.

My feet flew out from underneath me, and I grappled for anything to keep me from falling, but the only thing in reach was a pile of books which promptly fell on top of me. The books slamming to the ground and my shout of surprise caused the whole library to quieten.

As I moaned in pain, shifting the books off of me, a familiar haughty laugh filled my ears. "Looks like the first years this year aren't only stupid but clumsy," Sabrina crooned to her crew who giggled and pointed in my direction.

Dale knelt beside me and offered me a hand up all the while glaring at Sabrina and her table. Dale's disapproving gaze didn't have the same effect on Sabrina as with the other students. She simply wagged her fingers in his direction before going back to making a ruckus in the otherwise quiet library.

Anger and embarrassment filled my very being. Why did I even try to hide from her? What happened to my bravery? I stood up to her before and now because I tried to avoid confrontation, I made an even bigger idiot out of myself.

Finally scrambling to my feet with the help of Dale who also gathered my papers back up for me, I glowered at Sabrina who kept glancing back at me and giggling. I wouldn't let her get to me. I was bigger than that. *I'm the bigger person.*

Just then Sabrina started to imitate what I had looked like going down, wailing and flailing her hands. The others around her laughed and pointed in my direction.

Okay, no, I'm not. I'm not the bigger person.

I didn't know what I was doing, I'd never purposely tried to use magic, but I knew it was controlled by my emotions and the ball of light inside me. So, I grabbed all my anger and humiliation and focused on that light in my mind's eye. Stupid Sabrina Craftsman and her stupid big hair. Her perfect smile and her annoying friends. They weren't any better than anyone else. They weren't anything but a bunch of irritating birds. Squawking just for the sake of people hearing them.

There wasn't any kind of magical sparkle or glowing evidence of my spell, but there was something in the air. It thickened and crackled until suddenly ...

"Squawk!"

Sabrina jumped to her feet, her hands up in front of her face as she tried to get the words out of her mouth but all that would come were more varieties of squawking. Her friends hopped up and tried to comfort her, but they too could only squawk. Their faces reddened as they tried to get some kind of sentence out. The guys, who had only moments ago flaunted and flirted with them, tried to comfort them, but they soon started to exchange looks, and the laughter started.

Others in the library noticed Sabrina and her friend's predicament and, instead of trying to help, only laughed and giggled behind their books. A hand grabbed my elbow and dragged me out of the library before Sabrina could turn her squawk on me.

"That wasn't very smart," Dale told me once he had us out of the library and into the hallway. "Are you trying to paint a target on your back?"

Covering my mouth with my hand as I tried to hold back my laughter, I shook my head. "No, I'm sorry. I just couldn't help myself. She's such a—"

"Bitch. I know, but Sabrina is a Craftsman. You shouldn't poke at that snake. Especially if you're not going to claim your Mancaster name." Dale shook his head in disapproval, but the small smile on his lips showed he wasn't completely against my actions.

Lifting a shoulder, I grinned. "What can I say, I'm a beacon for trouble."

"Well, you better get that beacon turned off and fast." Dale poked me in the forehead, making me wince. "You're going to draw the wrong kind of attention, and with no official training, you're a sitting duck." He paused and stared down at me for a moment. "How did you do that, anyway?"

Starting back toward the quad, I lifted my hands in front of me. "Not really sure. I just thought she sounded like a bird the way she kept going on and on for anyone to hear and viola!" I grinned and flared my hands in front of me.

"While that was some impressive magic, only being able to cast spells when you're emotional is something a five-year-old would do. You need to get a hold of your abilities before you think about going head to head with anyone soon."

I thought about what Dale said and frowned. I really shouldn't have picked a fight when compared to Sabrina I was nothing more than a novice. I'd have to start improving and fast before she and her goons caught up with me again.

We made it back to the quad and the line of frozen students still waiting for Dale to come back. He didn't immediately go into the office. He seemed to want to say something to me but wasn't sure how to go about it.

105

"There's a lot more to show you, but I think today we should stop before you cause any more damage. Sabrina will no doubt figure out that spell came from you," Dale warned me, his eyes firmly on my face. "If I were you, I'd keep my head down and learn everything I can."

I nodded firmly. "Thanks. I will." I started to turn away but then spun back around. "Thanks again for showing me around. I know you didn't want to."

Dale flushed and adjusted his glasses, something I was beginning to think was some kind of nervous habit. "Don't worry about it. I needed a break from the line of idiots who have already lost their class schedules." When I raised a brow at him, holding my own class schedule close to my chest, Dale quickly added, "Not you obviously. Since it wasn't your fault. Anyway, I better unfreeze these guys before I lose my job and my scholarship." He started to shift away but then paused. "But first."

He closed his eyes for a moment, and the air felt thicker for some reason. Then all of a sudden everything was back to normal, and Dale opened his eyes. "There one blurred memory of your time in the office. You should be in the clear."

"Thanks."

"Think nothing of it. See ya."

I watched as Dale stalked back into the office, the line of students unfreezing the instant he was behind the desk, none of them the wiser that he'd been gone. I studied him for a few more moments. What an unusual guy, but at least I'd made another friend, a cute one at that.

With that thought, I made my way to the cafeteria where Trina was still eating. The moment she saw me, she started to wave me down. Walking toward her, I took in the dining area, which was set up with a buffet along one side and chairs and tables on the others.

"There you are. I got you a sandwich," Trina said, handing me a plastic wrapped sandwich as I sat down. "I thought you never were going to come. What happened in there?"

"You wouldn't believe me if I told you." I grinned at her as I unwrapped my sandwich. This was going to be an interesting school year, to say the least.

Chapter 8

THE FIRST DAY OF classes started like any other first day of school. I woke up, albeit begrudgingly, got dressed, and headed to breakfast with Trina, who thankfully also wasn't a morning person. Anyone who could be cheerful before ten o'clock was an alien life form in my book.

"So, what was life like back home?" Trina asked while we made our way through the breakfast line. "I mean, you went to a human school, right? That must have been cool."

I smiled at her as I grabbed an apple and put it on my tray. "Not really. It's like any other school." I paused for a moment, grabbing a cup of orange juice. "I mean, I'm not sure what magical schools are like. I mean besides this one, but humans schools are pretty much like this. You get up, go to school, go to class, socialize a bit in between. I mean, you have your cliques just like here, but the only difference really is that we don't have as many shortcuts for some of the mundane parts." I finished my explanation just as we stopped at the checkout. I handed my meal card to the lady behind the counter who swiped it and gave it back to me.

Trina led us through the tables until we found an open one. As we sat down with our meals, Trina asked, "But what about your mom? You never knew she was a witch? I mean, I'd find it hard not to do magic. You don't think I get this beautiful fro on my own, do you?" She puffed her hair up with a proud grin.

Laughing slightly, I took a drink of my juice before I answered. "No, she was good at hiding it, apparently. Or at least, I've never seen her use it." I tried to think back to any time she might have used magic without me knowing and came up blank.

"Maybe she wasn't using it," Trina offered up, dipping her spoon in her cereal. "If I were trying to stay out of the magic world, I would think that stopping cold turkey would be the way to go."

I hummed my agreement as I chewed my food. There were a lot of questions about mom and her life before dad and me that I hadn't had the chance to ask yet. I'd called her last night just like I'd promised, but our conversation more involved making sure I was doing okay and her getting to Cairo than a history of her life. I'd have to make a note to ask her about it some time.

"What about you? What's your family like?" I asked, trying to take the attention off of me. I still hadn't told Trina that my family was apparently of the elite variety. That wasn't something I really wanted to get into now. Especially since it might mean that I could lose one of my only friends at the school.

Trina grinned, more than happy to tell me all about her family. "I'm the youngest of two older sisters, both of which are perfect at everything." She rolled her eyes and groaned. "They can practically do no wrong, and both graduated with Sorcerer degrees."

"Sorcerer degrees?"

Trina's frowned. "Oh, yeah, sorry. I forget you are new to this. A Sorcerer degree is the highest level you can get in the school. Below that is a master's which takes four years, a Sorcerer takes six, and below that, there are the Practitioner degrees for those who are doing the bare minimum to get a decent job. Those only take a couple of years to get. Usually, those going into things like astronomy and herbology get those kinds." She clearly found them to be some of the less desirable subjects.

"Understood." I nodded though it was quite a bit of information to swallow before breakfast was over. "What about friends back home? Any special someone's you left behind?"

A small grin crept up Trina's face answering the question for me. "Well, there is this one person that I liked, but I don't know if they liked me or not. I mean we did kiss at a party once, but it could have been nothing." She shrugged and tried to play it off.

"You kissed?" I gasped, leaning on my elbow as I tried to urge her to tell me more. "That has to mean something."

Trina waved a hand in the air and shook her head. "Nah, I'm sure it was nothing. She's not like that." She seemed a bit deflated to admit it. For sure, Trina like this person more than she wanted to admit. Turning the attention off of her, Trina asked, "So, what about you? Friends? Lovers? Tell me the deets."

Giggling, I waved her off. "No lovers. Not anymore anyway. But I do have a best friend. Callie. She's like a sister to me."

Nodding eagerly to hear more, Trina asked, "So what'd she think when she found out you're a witch?"

Brows furrowed, I stared at her. "I didn't tell her."

"What? If she's your best friend, I'd find it hard not to tell her." Trina stabbed her cereal with her spoon.

A bit perturbed at my lack of secret divulging to my human best friend, I grumbled, "I was told it was against the rules."

"Well, technically it is." Trina lifted her spoon in the air, her eyes lifted to the sky as she thought. "But who else would you break the rules for? I mean, I'd do it in a heartbeat for the right person."

I frowned at her explanation, my stomach starting to twist into knots at her words. Callie was my best friend. We told each other everything. She knew the moment I had sex with Jaron and was there to help me eat a whole pint of ice cream as I cried over him and his asshole excuse. If she hadn't proved herself trustworthy by now, I didn't know what would ever do it.

Thinking about Callie made me realize I hadn't called her at all since messaging her yesterday. She probably thought I had fallen off the face of the earth.

Pulling my phone out of my pocket, I stood up. "Uh, I'll meet you at lunch. I need to make a call."

Trina waved me off as I rushed out of the cafeteria and onto the open terrace next to the dining. Quickly hitting Callie's name on my phone, I waited with anxiety bubbling through me as the phone rang. What would I tell her? Would she even believe me? The longer it took for her to answer the more nervous I became, and I almost hung up just as a groggy voice came on the line.

"Hello?"

"Hey, Callie." I tucked one hand into the pocket of my shorts and leaned into the phone.

"Max! Is that you?" Callie's half-asleep voice transformed into a high-pitched squeal. "Oh my god, I thought you'd been kidnapped by some sex traffickers or worse, forced to work in a sweatshop where they make those really cute but really shoddy shoes!"

I smiled at her ridiculous accusations and shook my head. Remembering she couldn't see me, I said into the phone, "No, I'm fine. I'm actually not at my grandma's house like I said."

"I knew it!" Callie shouted, making me wince. "You lying hussy. You thought you could pull one over me, but I knew you weren't there because your phone GPS says you're still in Atlanta."

"You traced my phone?" I gaped, and half laughed.

Callie sobered slightly. "Well, the app was still on my phone from that one time you lost it when we went to the state fair. I would be a bad best friend if I didn't check up on you. By the way, why didn't you tell me you were going to some hoity-toity college here? What about Brown?"

I sighed and tried to figure out how to tell her the most mind-blowing information of her lifetime. "I'm sorry about Brown. I really had every intention of going, but my mom dropped this bombshell on me, something about our family and how we all went to this college over here and well ..."

"You caved," Callie finished for me with a sound of finality. "It's understandable. I mean, you don't know anything about her family. Of course, you'd want to get closer to her side. Maybe even meet your grandparents. I guess the hotties there are just as good as the hotties at Brown."

"Callie ..." I tried to interrupt her, but she would not be stopped.

"There's only so many things one can expect of a best friend before they have to spread their wings and find their own way," she mock-sniffled as if she were going to cry. "Fly, little birdie, fly."

"Callie, I'm a witch!" I shouted into the phone and then quickly glanced around me. A couple of students on their way to the cafeteria stopped and stared at me, but nobody came running to arrest me for my declaration.

"Sure, you're a witch. You left your best friend to go to college on her own so that you could go to some rich people school." Callie sniffled again. "I get it. It's cool. I just hope you remember me when you're married to a Senator and I'm shaking my tits down at the strip club trying to make ends meet."

Rolling my eyes at Callie's dramatic turn, I huddled into my phone and hissed, "Shut up. You couldn't be a stripper if you wanted to."

"Could too. I might not have the boobs, but have you seen my butt? You could pop a quarter off that thing!"

"Callie, I'm serious. I'm a real witch. I'm talking pointing hats, riding broomsticks – actually, that part I'm not sure is real - but remember when Jaron caught on fire at graduation?" I paused for her to confirm that she remembered. "That was me! And the soda cans exploding at my party too. I'm a flippin' modern-day Charmed One!"

There was silence on the other line for a moment. I had to look at the phone to make sure I hadn't lost her before the line filled with laughter.

"Oh. My. God. Max, you almost got me." She giggled hysterically. "Like you could cause Jaron to spontaneously catch on fire. He was smoking like the teachers said."

"Yeah, the same Jaron who's dead against smoking and wouldn't jeopardize his chances of keeping his football scholarship by picking it up on graduation day!"

Callie went quiet for a moment but then slowly said, "Okay, say I believe you. Say you are in fact a witch. Prove it."

I glanced around me and then threw up my free hand. "How the heck am I supposed to do that? I can't control the crap let alone show you over the phone." A clock dinged in the distance reminding me I was about to be late for class. "Look, I have class until four, meet me at the gates and we can go somewhere, and I'll show you. Okay?"

Letting out a huff of breath, Callie clipped, "Fine, but you better not be trying to pull a fast one on me because I'm not one of those wild theorists. I have my standards and a hardcore Christian mom who would kill me if she found out my best friend was Satan's spawn."

Bursting out laughing, I quickly promised once more to meet her later before hanging up the phone. Shaking my head, I headed back into the building. I wasn't sure how I was going to show Callie that I was a witch. Like I'd told her, I wasn't exactly in control of my abilities, but I'd have to think of something. Maybe I'd bring a textbook with me? Or even my class schedule. Would that be proof enough?

Either way, I'd have to think about it later because at that moment I had *A Magical History* to get to and I was already going to be late. What a sorry witch I was turning out to be.

Chapter 9

I RAN DOWN THE hallway toward my first class of the day. A Magical History. Not that I was particularly fond of history, but I had a feeling any kind of history dealing with magic had to be better than learning of about the Great Gold Rush of 1849.

When I arrived, the door was already closed. Without knocking, I threw the door open and darted into the room. My feet froze to the floor as six sets of eyes fell on me. Adjusting my book bag on my shoulder, I awkwardly shifted in place.

"Don't just stand there, take a seat." The older man at the front of the room, who I could only assume was my new teacher, glared at me and waited with arms crossed for me to do as he said.

Ducking my head down, I quickly found a seat in the many open seats, trying to make myself as small as possible. As the professor started again, I noticed the name on the chalkboard. Professor Piston.

"Now, as I was saying," Professor Piston drawled, "we don't offer this course to very many students as you can see by the small attendance." He gestured around the room with an increasingly annoyed expression. Obviously, he wasn't teaching this class by choice.

I shifted in my seat, feeling even more out of place. The others seemed just as uncomfortable, like we were unwanted in our own classroom. My first day of classes wasn't starting off too well.

"Most of our students here learned all they need to know about how the magical community came to be when they were in their diapers." Professor Piston pushed his glasses up his nose, shooting us a condescending glower. "Despite my protests, the Headmaster has found it necessary to allow students who have not acquired the required education before allowing them into our prestigious school."

Please tell us how you really feel. I crossed my arms over my chest and forced myself to hold my tongue. One thing I hated more than bullies were judgmental assholes and Professor Piston was well on his way to finding his way onto my shit list.

Professor Piston picked up the book titled *A Magical History* and waved it in the air. "I expect every single one of you had a chance to read the textbook for this class already. I won't be coddling anyone who didn't do the homework."

Homework? Who assigns homework before the class even begins! And as if my day couldn't get any worse, the door to the classroom opened up and in walked in Paul, my deliciously beautiful Adonis who had helped me with my bags yesterday.

"Ah, Paul, there you are." Professor Piston let his scathing look of distaste for us dissipate momentarily to give Paul a respectful nod.

"Sorry for the delay. Here are the papers you wanted copied." Paul grinned at Professor Piston, showing a dimple in his cheek I hadn't noticed before, and suddenly I was shifting uncomfortably in my seat for a whole other reason.

Professor Piston snorted, his nose flaring unpleasantly. "No fault of yours. That imbecile working the office wouldn't know a replica spell from a transmogrifying spell." He took the papers from Paul's hands and sat them on his desk before turned back to the classroom. "Class, this is my teacher's aide, Paul. He will be helping me transform you mediocre excuses for magical beings into respectful, working members of our society. Though I hold no such high hopes for such a result, alas, we must move forward. Please open your book to page five where we will now discuss the rise and fall of the idiotic being who calls himself a wizard, Merlin."

While the professor continued to rant about how Merlin barely constituted as a magical being, let alone the greatest wizard of all time, my eyes were set on Paul. He had taken a seat at a table not too far away from Professor Piston's. His eyes were down on the papers on his desk, the dark brown of his hair falling into his eyes as he read. My eyes followed his every movement from the way he touched his pen to his lower lip to his brow furrowing in concentration. When his eyes moved up from his paper and met mine, my breath caught in my chest. Very slowly, a grin spread across his lips, causing things low inside of me to tighten.

As I started to remember how to breathe, a shadow cast itself over my desk, but I hardly noticed. The book slamming into the table in front of me, however, made me jump, my eyes ripping away from Paul and to a snarling Professor Piston. My face flushed red as I realized everyone in the room was looking at me.

"If you are quite finished ogling my assistant, tell me, Miss ...?" He stared down at me, and I realized he expected me to tell him my name.

"Norman. Max Norman."

Apparently, my name did not impress the professor by the way his nose curled up his face. "Well, then Miss Norman, since you find no need to pay attention to my lecture, why don't you tell us who the most profound magical member of the wizarding society today is?"

My mouth fell open, and I gaped like a fish. My mind raced as I tried to think of some modern-day witch or wizard but the only name I could think of was my own mother, and I wasn't about to point that one out.

"We're waiting, Miss Norman." He spat my name like it tasted foul in his mouth.

Finally, giving up, I bowed my head and shook it. "I don't know."

Professor Piston scowled. "Of course, you don't. You also probably haven't read the textbook either, have you?"

"No, professor," I admitted, my face becoming redder by the second with pure humiliation.

"If you had, you would know that Xander Craftsman has won that award the last five years running, having revolutionized—"

"The way we do spell work," I interrupted him, having heard it a million times already.

Professor Piston pressed his lips together tightly and narrowed his eyes at me. "Yes, precisely, and for future reference, do not interrupt me while I am speaking. And eyes off my assistant. This is a place to educate your mind, not your raging hormones." He gave me one more admonishing look before moving back to the head of the class. From then on, I kept my eyes down or on the professor, resisting the urge to look at Paul even though I could feel his eyes on me.

The class dragged on, and by the time the bell chimed the hour, I was more than ready to be on to my next class. I just hoped all the professors weren't as dull and rude as Piston, or I might have to rethink my position on Brown.

After I gathered my things and headed for the door, I found a body blocking my path. My eyes trailed up the hard planes underneath the blue cotton shirt and up to the dreamy chocolate brown eyes. Those kissable lips curved into a smirk that made me weak in the knees.

"Max, right?"

I swallowed thickly and licked my dry lips before stuttering out, "Yeah, Max. And you're Paul."

"Right." Paul grinned broadly either because of my clear nervousness, or he thought I was mentally disabled. It could have been either, really. We stood there for a moment before Paul asked, "Do you want me to walk you to your next class? If you're taking Piston, you probably have Mystial next, right?"

"Yes, I do." I nodded so hard I thought my head would fall off my neck. Forcing myself not to seem so overeager, I shrugged a shoulder. "Sure, if you want to."

Simply smiling at me, Paul took my bag from my hands before I could protest and started down the hall. I followed after him, my shorter legs barely keeping up with his long strides. Not wanting to let it get awkward again, I scrounged up the little courage I had as I turned to him.

"So, do you go here?"

Paul glanced my way and chuckled. "Yes, I go here. I'm only a teaching assistant during my off periods. As a third year, you are required to assist one professor each semester. It's their way of making us learn responsibility by giving back to the school."

I thought back to Professor Piston's class and frowned. "I think I'd have rather picked up trash than assist Piston."

Suddenly, Paul threw his head back and laughed, a glorious sound that fluttered through my body, making every nerve come alive. I could listen to him laugh all day.

"Professor Piston isn't as bad as he seems. He just doesn't like lazy people or anything really to do with people at all. He only likes me because I laugh at his jokes." Paul glanced back my way, his dimple showing once more.

"Well, I didn't even know about the reading assignment. It's hardly my fault."

Paul gave me a quizzical look. "It was in your welcome packet, wasn't it?"

I let out a growl that startled Paul. "Sorry, I didn't mean to growl, but I didn't get that either until just yesterday. Something about the Headmaster wanting to meet me."

"Why would he want to do that?" Paul cocked his head to the side in the most adorable way.

I scrambled for an excuse that didn't involve me telling him my family's magical last name. For a moment, I was tempted to tell him. I wanted to impress this guy for some reason, something I blame completely on my raging hormones.

Not coming up with a good excuse, I shrugged. "Beats me. He just wanted to chat."

"That's strange." Paul's brow furrowed. "The headmaster doesn't usually bother with anyone but the top families. You know, the ones who can benefit the school."

Not wanting to be caught in a lie, I chose to stay quiet. Instead, I chose to focus on the area around us. Quite a few students were making their way through the hallway on their way to class. It wouldn't be an anomaly had most of their eyes not been on Paul and me. In fact, it seemed everyone was watching us.

I would understand the stares at Paul. He was worth staring at. But there were definitely people eyeballing me as well. And whispering. Something was definitely up.

"Why are they staring?" I asked as we stopped before the open door of the room I knew was Professor Mystial's. I'd been excited to start this class since it would for sure be one that had some kind of magical work in it and not just reading about it. However, my excitement was trumped by the ominous stares.

Paul glanced around us as if just noticing the attention we were receiving. With a shrug and a grin, Paul turned his gaze back to me. "Who knows? But if I were them, I'd be staring at you too."

"Why? Do I have something on my face?" I touched my cheek and then swiped the back of my hand over it just in case some of my breakfast had still lingered there.

He let out another one of those skin-tingling chuckles and brushed my hair behind my ear. "See you later, Max." His eyes then went to the door, and his smile wilted slightly. "Sabrina."

Sabrina's blue eyes gleamed as she grinned broadly at Paul and placed her hand on his arm, moving in as close to him as possible. "Hi, Paul. I was wondering when I was going to see you. Have you been avoiding me?"

Inwardly, I cheered at how Paul's posture tensed up. On the outside, I watched with passive boredom as if their exchange meant nothing to me. I actually was going berserk to know what was going on between the two of them.

"Was I being too subtle about it?" Paul gave her a tight smile before moving out of her grasp. "I thought I was quite obvious."

Sabrina pouted. "Ah, Paulie. You're not still upset about what happened with your brother, are you? I told you, it was nothing. Just a drunken fling. Plus we were broken up at the time." She moved in closer once more and trailed her fingers up Paul's chest.

Paul caught her hand in his and shoved it back at her. "I don't have time for this." Turning back to me, Paul gave me a soft smile. "Sorry, Max."

Grinning like a cat that ate the canary, I waved him off. "Don't worry about it. See you in class."

I watched him walk away until he was out of sight, and I had to acknowledge the glowering diva in front of me. With her arms crossed over her chest, Sabrina tapped her fingers on her arm. "Can I help you?" I asked her.

"Stay away from Paul." Sabrina stepped closer so that we were nose-to-nose. "He's off limits. In fact, stay away from any of the guys here. You aren't worthy of their attention, you filthy little pretender." She whipped her hair over her shoulder as she left, hitting me in the face with it. I was instantly engulfed in the strong fragrance of her shampoo, or maybe it was her perfume. Either way, she had drenched herself in it, and I almost coughed up a lung trying to get out of it.

"You should listen to her, you know," a small voice told me after I finally stopped coughing. I shifted my gaze to the person talking. The brunette who had been with Sabrina the other day stood there, a pitying expression in her eyes. "Sabrina can be vicious. Especially about her exes."

"And Paul is one of those, I take it?"

"Not one of them, the one." The brunette nodded firmly. "They are always on again, off again, but everyone knows they will eventually get back together. They're destined for each other." The way she said it was like it was some deep dark secret she wasn't supposed to divulge. The fact that she had told me made me wonder if she wasn't as bad as Sabrina seemed.

"I don't think we were introduced." I held my hand out to her. "I'm Max."

The brunette smiled and took my hand. "Monica Magenski. My mother invented the high-temperature cauldron. They're spelled never to burn no matter how long you are away from them." She beamed with so much pride that I had to smile back.

"Nice to meet you," I told her as we moved into the classroom. "And I think I got one of your mom's cauldrons. My mom picked it out, so I can't be sure. I'm pretty new to all this." I sat my stuff down at one of the tables. This classroom was set up like a chemistry lab with charts and Bunsen-burner-like stations.

"Oh, you're one of those kids."

I tilted my head to the side curious at her wording. "What kids?"

Monica quickly explained, "Enders. Those whose parents waited until they absolutely had to tell you about your magical roots. So, tell me, did you blow something up?"

I flushed at her question. "Yeah, sort of."

"Not surprised." Monica giggled and waved a hand at me. "Most Enders end up blowing something up."

"Why do you call them Enders?"

Before Monica could answer, a throat cleared, and our eyes went to a woman in her mid-forties with her hair twisted tightly on top of her head. *Must be Professor Mystial.* I made a show of opening my book as Monica moved around the desk, starting to head back to where Sabrina and the other blonde girl sat. When Professor Mystial turned toward the board, she darted back to my side.

"They're called Enders because they often end in disaster," she whispered quickly and then winked at me before skipping back to her spot.

Frowning down at my book, I thought about what Monica had said. Enders. The magical community obviously didn't have high expectations for late bloomers, which was all we were. I hadn't done anything bad

130

enough yet to deserve the name Ender. I mean, I wasn't going to end in a disaster. I might not be a perfect student, but whenever I put my mind to it, I always excel at what I do. Magic would be no different, and I would prove it to them. Well, right after I figured out how to control my powers.

Chapter 10

PROFESSOR MYSTIAL'S CLASS WAS better and worse than Professor Piston's. While she didn't go on and on about a bunch of dead guys who may or may not have been frauds, she was very aggressive in her teaching.

Whenever someone got the answer wrong, she would snipe at them, pointing out what exactly they were doing wrong and announcing it for the whole class to hear. Unfortunately, Potions 101 was a full class, and so when I almost burnt my eyebrows off from mixing too much hydroxy to the newt and sulfur concoction, everyone knew about it.

Sabrina and her crew cackled like hyenas in the back of the room, pointing and jeering. Monica laughed as well but not quite as much as the rest of them. The blonde with large eyes and even larger breasts, whose name I learned in class was Libby Moreling, seemed perfectly content to go along with anything that Sabrina said or did. A sheep if I ever saw one.

"No, Norman." Professor Mystial scowled and jerked the stirring spoon out of my hand. "You must stir it counterclockwise, or the ingredients don't blend in harmony."

"What's the difference?" I asked, quite fed up with being corrected. A collection of gasps pulled my attention away from the professor and then over to others in the class. Each and every one of them had a shocked expression on their faces, well, except for Sabrina who only laughed.

Professor Mystial cleared her throat, drawing my attention back to her. "The difference is whether or not you actually create a drought of longevity or blowing up the entire lab." She shoved the stirring spoon back into my hand. "Now, pay attention. I'd hate to lose a student on the first day."

Frowning hard, I forced back the tears of frustration burning my eyes. I stirred counterclockwise as my other hand clutched the counter in front of me. I thought this experience was going to be, you know, magical. That I would learn how to turn teacups into frogs, or maybe how to levitate something, but all I had learned so far was how stupid I was for coming here in the first place.

"Don't feel so bad," Monica murmured as she stopped at the counter next to me to pick up more newt. "Everyone asks that question at the beginning."

"Really?" I blinked back my tears and glanced at her out of the corner of my eye. Sabrina was busy talking the other girl's ear off and didn't notice Monica hanging around me longer than needed.

"Yeah, and Sabrina once told me she went bald in third grade because of a potion went awry." Monica giggled quietly, and I grinned in return.

"Thanks, Monica."

"No problem." Monica waved at me before hurrying back to where Sabrina sat.

Monica's words made me not feel so bad. I wasn't a complete idiot. I was behind everyone else, and it would be obvious I had a lot to learn. You would think that if a student were in beginner classes, the teachers would have more sympathy for those who didn't learn this stuff at birth.

For the rest of the class, I made sure to do everything exactly as the book said and hung on Mystial's every word. Thankfully, I was able to get out of class without any more mishaps. Not that Sabrina wasn't looking for them. Her eyes were boring into my back most of the class. As we were getting ready to leave, she made a point to walk by my table and 'accidentally' knock my books off the table.

"Oops, sorry." Sabrina grinned but didn't offer to help me pick them up as she sauntered out of the classroom.

I let out an aggravated sigh as I knelt to pick up my things. I took me a bit longer than I expected since my pens rolled under the side table. I had to lie down on my stomach and stretch my arm beneath the table to reach them.

When I stood up, someone else was at my table. The large, intimidating man I ran into back at the administration office stood at my table. He stared down at my things, still sitting on the table with a confused look on his face.

"Can I help you?" I asked, creeping up to the table slowly as if I were approaching a twitchy animal.

The large man glanced up at me and then back to my things. "This is my table."

My eyes shot to the clock on the wall. It wasn't even time for the next class yet. It was actually lunch time. Why was this guy menacing at me when he should be feeding his overly large body mass?

Not willing to test whether or not he was actually hungry and might be tempted to eat me, I went the less sarcastic road. "I'm sorry, I'll be gone in a moment." I grabbed my things and shoved them back into my bag, the entire time watching me with his piercing stare.

I hurried along the longer he stared. When I finally had my things together, I met his stare with one of my own. "I'm going now."

He didn't say anything but then, without warning, sat down at the table where my things used to be, completely ignoring me. My eyes trailed over his large muscular form once more. The way his t-shirt with some kind of game character on the front clung to his thick biceps and stretched across his chest. His jeans fitted tight to his legs and butt, and I had to force myself not to tilt my head to get a better look.

Finally noticing my staring, the mountain of a man shifted his eyes to my direction, and I was instantly drowned in cerulean blues. My mouth slowly hung open, and all I could do was stare with no regard for appropriateness. I had seen this guy before but only briefly. I hadn't had the chance to take him fully in until just now. The beautiful mountain of a man was quite something to behold. Even more so when he opened his gorgeous mouth to speak once more.

"Are you alright?"

Licking my lips, my mouth suddenly dry, I shook my head. "Ah, no. I'm fine. Just lost in thought." More like raging libido.

"I can call the healer." His eyes bore into me intensely, not accepting my explanation.

I slung my bag over my shoulder and held my hands up, waving him off. "No, no. I'm really fine. No need to get the healer involved." I knocked the side of my head and chuckled. "Just a bit of first day of school jitters."

The man watched me quietly before nodding once and turning away from me.

With his intense gaze off of me, I walked two steps toward the door. Before I got to the door for some reason, I stopped and spun around. "By the way, I'm Max."

Those crystalline blues locked onto me once more and that small hint of a smile tugged on the side of his lips. I thought he might not answer me and had already half turned away to bury my head in the sand when he said, "Aidan."

My head twisted back to him, and I smiled. "Hello, Aidan."

As I went through the rest of my day, I couldn't stop thinking about the people I'd met since I had started Winchester Academy, more importantly, the men I'd met. Callie was going to be so jealous. If she thought the hotties at Brown were something to drool over, then she would go gaga when I told her about the ones here right in Georgia.

I ran my bag back up to my room just as my phone beeped.

Callie: I'm at the gates. Douche bag guard won't let me pass without a pass.

Me: I'm sorry, I forgot. You have to get one from the headmaster.

Callie: You mean, I have to kiss some old dude's ass to visit you? BS.

Laughing as I shook my head, I tucked my phone in my pocket and headed back toward the front of the school. As I walked down the hallway, my hands shook at my sides as I clenched and unclenched them. My nerves from before about Callie and lying about school came rushing back.

I caught sight of Callie's bright cherry red '65 convertible, and my heart beat even faster in my chest. I remembered the summer she had spent rebuilding the rust bucket of a car with her dad. Well, more like I remembered her bitching and moaning about how long it was taking. However, the end result had far outweighed the man-hours.

Opening the door and sliding into the dark leather seat, I smiled weakly at Callie. "Hey."

Callie turned her head my way, her large black sunglasses covering half of her face and tangled in her dark, windblown hair. "Well, look who it is. Our very own Samantha Stevenson. How are things in the magical community? Change anyone into a frog today?"

"Shh!" I jumped across the seat and slapped my hands over her mouth, my eyes wide as I searched around for witnesses. "You can't just say that crap out loud." A wet muscle touched the palm of my hand, and I jerked my hand back. "Did you just lick me?"

"Yes, I did, and you're lucky that's all I did." Callie sniffed, putting her nose in the air. "And what's going to happen? Some Death Eaters going to come silence me?" She threw her head back and laughed as if this was all a game and nothing serious would ever happen to her.

I pinched her arm and stared hard at her until she stopped laughing.

"You're serious." She pulled off her sunglasses, her brows knitting together as she searched my face.

"Like seventh-grade homeroom serious." I leveled my gaze on her, reminding her of the one time that she had gotten her period in homeroom and was wearing pale pink pants at the time. To say the humiliation she would have felt had I not worn a sweater that day was unmeasurable. She'd have been scarred for life and sure as hell wouldn't have gotten that date with Bobby Flinn.

"Seventh-grade serious, huh?" Callie sighed and put her sunglasses back on. "Alright then. Let's get something to eat. I feel like I'm going to need a chocolate milkshake for this story." She cranked the car, and as we pulled away from the curb, I had a sinking feeling in my gut. I wasn't sure what it was, but it wasn't something a chocolate milkshake would fix.

The next few minutes on our way to our favorite burger and shake joint, The Burger Shack, we acted as if there wasn't this huge secret between us. We blared the music on the radio and sang at the top of our lungs. For a moment, it was just like any other time we hung out. Just for a moment. Then we pulled into the parking lot, and everything began to sink back in.

Climbing out of the car, my feet moved on their own accord, going through the motions of entering the front door and finding a seat in the red vinyl booth. I grabbed a menu from behind the salt and pepper shakers and hid my face as I pretended that I would get something other than my usual burger and fry combo with a chocolate milkshake.

Fingers curled around the top half of my menu and pulled down, revealing Callie's impatient face.

"Hello?" Callie asked, putting her sunglasses on top of her head. "Are you going to just ignore me the whole time?"

Sighing, I sat my menu down on the table. "No, I'm not. I'm just trying to get my thoughts together. It's not every day you have to tell your best friend you're a freak of nature."

Callie snorted. "Too late for that. I've been thinking that since day one."

I rolled my eyes. "Thanks a lot."

"But seriously ..." Callie shifted forward in her seat. "Are we talking Harry Potter or Charmed? Finger wagging or swish and flick?" I'd have thought she was joking had there not been such an eagerness in her voice.

Before I could open my mouth to answer her, our waitress stopped at the table. "Hey girls, what can I get for you today?"

"Oh, Rosie." Callie grinned. "You know, you don't need to ask us that."

Rosie, a late twenties strawberry blonde with a five-year-old son at home, always waited on our table. We both ordered the same thing every time, but still, she asked us without fail.

"And you know I have to ask, or my boss will get up my butt." She winked, and we giggled in unison. "So, what will it be?"

Callie spouted off our usuals. Two cheeseburgers and fries with two chocolate shakes, extra onions on Callie's cheeseburger. How she stood the taste of them, I'd never know.

"So ..." Callie clasped her hands in front of her and leaned forward in her seat. "Spill. Are the wizard hotties better than the Brown hotties you are leaving me alone with?"

I grinned and chuckled at her ridiculous question. I knew it was coming, and yet it surprised me. Immediately, my mind went to the most recent guy who had caught my eye. Aidan. Tall, mysterious with muscles I'd love to get wrapped up in.

"I knew it!" Callie shouted, pointing a finger at me drawing several patrons eyes toward us. "You are holding out on me."

I shook my head and forced back a grin. "I'm not, I swear. There are surprisingly quite a few 'hotties' though none that have outright showed interest in me." My mind immediately called me a liar, giving me a full-blown image of Ian, winking and smirking as he left the administrator's office. Ian didn't have to be in the office, and yet he had hung around because I was there.

Callie peered at me curiously. "Wait a moment. There is someone! Who? Who? Tell me everything."

"I thought you wanted to know about the school, not about my love life?" I cocked a brow at her and then turned my attention to Rosie, who sat our milkshakes down in front of us.

"Here you girls go, anything else I can get you at the moment?"

"No, we're good," I told Rosie, taking a long, cold, and sugary drink of my shake. When Rosie was gone, I started again, anxious to get it over with. "So, no wand-waving, and no finger-pointing. At least, not yet. I haven't really gotten a chance to cast a spell or anything. It's been a lot of book work. I did make a potion though it didn't quite turn out right." I made a face as I remembered the gunky mess I'd created during Potions 101.

"So, can you show me something?" Callie asked, sucking on her straw and staring at me. I was beginning to feel a bit like a circus freak.

I thought about it for a moment. None of the things I'd tried to do over the summer had worked. The only thing I'd managed to do was give myself a headache. Yesterday in the library had been my first and only real, on-purpose magic, and all I did was make Sabrina and her lackeys squawk like a bird. What could I possibly do here in the diner where anyone could see me without getting caught?

My mind whirled while I tried to think of something and then the bell of the diner door dinged. Automatically, my eyes went to the door, and they settled on a red-brown mop of hair.

"Dale!" I cried out without meaning to, causing him to look in our direction. Suddenly, I wanted to crawl into a hole and hide. I didn't mean to call his attention, I was just so shocked to see another magical person in somewhere so ordinary as The Burger Shack. Which was ridiculous since they were probably going here long before I ever went. Just because I now knew about them didn't give me any claim to the human-world places. But still, it was strange to see my two lives mixing before my eyes.

"Hey, Max." Dale stopped in front of our table his eyes going from me to Callie. "You like this place too, huh?"

"Oh, yeah," I said lamely, smacking myself mentally.

"I'm Callie, Max's best friend," my best friend said, turning her eyes on Dale, obvious interest gleaming in them.

"Nice to meet you." Dale nodded curtly but didn't seem much interested in her otherwise.

Not to be ignored, Callie flicked a hand at Dale. "So, do you go to that special school like Max?"

All of a sudden, I realized the danger of this situation. Callie wasn't supposed to know about me being a witch or anything about the school. Here I was, flaunting her in front of one of the school's workers. Dale worked only a few feet away from the Headmaster after all. If he found out that I told Callie, then he could get me in serious trouble.

My heart beat rapidly in my chest as I tried to figure out how to get out of the precarious situation I'd gotten myself into. A loud pop caused me and everyone around me to startle, and then a warm red goop landed on Callie and me, coating the table until it looked like a murder scene. I froze in place, my eyes going from the plastic ketchup bottle that had exploded to Dale's face. The expression of horror was exactly identical to my own, and I knew I was in for it.

"Oh, my." Rosie hurried over and handed both Callie and me a wet rag while she started to wipe off the table. "Talk about a freak accident, huh?"

Callie and I exchanged a look and then promptly busted out laughing. Dale did not look as amused as we were and simply shook his head while watching.

"Well, I guess that's one way to prove it." Callie giggled as she dabbed at her face, the ketchup really giving her a Carrie kind of vibe.

"Sorry," I muttered as Rosie rushed off to get another wash rag. "Those kinds of things keep happening to me. It's really a pain."

"I can imagine." Callie nodded and grinned. "Can't be good for you or the condiments."

I met her grin with one of my own, but it fell as Dale came back in front of us.

"This really is no laughing matter." Arms crossed over his button-up shirt, Dale's lips pressed into a hard line and I swore if he glared any harder his eyes would pop out of his sockets.

"Oh, please. Chill out. It's ketchup, not the White House." Callie giggled and flipped her hair, grimacing as her hand came in contact with even more red goop.

Dale ignored Callie and turned his gaze to me. "Today might be ketchup, but tomorrow, it could very well be the whole city."

I shrunk into my seat at his words, knowing in some ways that it was true. If I

146

didn't get a hold of my magic and emotions, I could very well end up hurting someone for real.

"Oh god, listen to this guy." Callie rolled her eyes. "But he does have a point." She tapped her chin in thought and then point it at me. "What happens the next time you get your period? You have a massive PMS attack, and you blow up the person you're mad at?"

"Callie," I warned and sighed, but it was no use.

"Or, or ..." Callie smacked the table repeatedly. "What if you're having sex and right when you orgasm, you cause a massive earthquake?"

"Oh, God. Please stop!" I buried my face in my hand, my cheeks no doubt as red as the ketchup in my hair. I didn't dare look up and see Dale's expression though I was sure it was probably as horrified as mine.

"Just think about it," Callie continued as if none of us had said anything. "You can officially claim that you had rocked his world."

Merlin, shoot me now.

Chapter 11

I COVERED MY MOUTH as I yawned for what felt like the millionth time. It wasn't that the class I was sitting in was boring. On the contrary, Charmology was one of the classes I had most been looking forward too. Sure, it was a beginner's course, something I would have taken in grade school but being a late bloomer, I needed all the help I could get.

"Charms can be very precocious. One mispronunciation and your love charm will turn into a hex," my professor, Calliope no-last-name's whimsical voice explained as she sort of floated around the room. She was much younger than the other professors I'd seen, her fair skin almost shimmered in the light, and her hair trailed after her like a separate piece of herself. While Calliope's voice was very nice to listen to, it did nothing for my tired eyes.

I'd already had two lattes from the cafeteria by the time I had finished breakfast. Trina had tried to make small talk with me, but I hadn't been coherent enough really to answer more than a yes or no, maybe a few hmms. I'd spent all night tossing and turning over what had happened at The Burger Shack.

After my little exploding ketchup trick, Dale hadn't said much, not about my accident or about Callie and the fact that she obviously knew what we were. The only thing he had left me with was a despairing sigh and a head shake before he left the diner, leaving Callie and me alone to clean up the mess.

I kept expecting Dale to show up wanting an explanation or the headmaster telling me I was expelled not just from school but from life. But neither of those things ever came. While it was driving me crazy to find out what Dale was going to do with the information, I was hard-pressed to not rock that boat. If he wasn't saying anything, I wasn't saying anything.

Thankfully, Callie was the queen of secrets. I didn't have to worry about her cracking, even under pain of torture or death. I trusted her with my life, and I knew she would keep my secret. If only I could do a better job at it.

Something cold pressed against the side of my arm, and then a hot jolt of electricity went through my entire body. My eyes, which I hadn't even known I'd closed, flew open, and any sleepiness I might have felt went flying from me as the class stared at me with open amusement.

After a moment, the hot shock of energy that had ripped through me dissipated. I gasped and blinked rapidly as my chest moved up and down trying to catch my breath.

"And that, class, is an energizer charm."

My head turned, and my chin lifted to meet the eyes of Calliope, who held a metal coin with a strange swirl in the middle in between her fingers. A small smile covered her lips as she watched me watch her. Surprisingly, there wasn't a hint of annoyance on her face, only simple amusement.

"Sorry," I ducked my head in embarrassment and apology.

"No worries. We all have issues getting up and going in the morning. That's why these charms are so important," Calliope continued, speaking to the class as she floated around the room, her gown fluttering along her feet. "I will teach you how to create such a thing for yourselves and for others. Though, if you decide to become a merchant of such objects, you will need at least a master's degree as well as quite a few legal documents, insurance and such." She paused for a moment and smiled. "In every customer service position, there's always that one person who cannot be satisfied no matter what you do. You need to cover yourself and your assets."

It sounded way more business-like than something they would talk about it magic school. I expected everything here to be all fairy dust and finger twitching, but there weren't that many occurrences of magic, even in the hallways. Dale had done more magic than any of the others I'd seen besides my accidentally-on-purpose mishaps with Sabrina and then Callie. It wasn't that I wasn't loving being there and learning as much as possible. I was just expecting ... more.

Someone raised their hand, drawing my attention out of my inner thoughts and back to class.

"Yes?" Calliope pointed to the blonde boy who had raised his hand.

"So, you can just make a charm for anything?" His eyes were full of hope and eagerness. It made his next words hardly surprising. "I can make myself taller? Luckier? More charming?" He shifted in his seat as the class giggled and laughed at his words. I could see how the lanky boy might want those things. He probably hadn't been able to get a date and was dying to try out his newfound abilities on the local beauties.

After the class settled down from their initial reaction, all eyes turned to Calliope. Though none of us had been brave enough to ask, we had all wanted to what the rules were, how far we could go before we were getting cuffed and thrown out on our asses.

Calliope watched us all. Her smile never wilted, but the way her eyes hardened made us all stiffen in our seats. "There are many things one can do with magic. You could make yourself appear however you wish. Taller. Smaller. Even more attractive. You could make yourself rich beyond your wildest dreams."

These words made a few people smile and relax a bit. Calliope was saying all the right things, but I wasn't naïve enough to know there wasn't a catch. There was always a catch.

"However ..." That single word resonated throughout the classroom, killing any whispers or giggles. "Magic has a price. Many of you might have noticed that ball of energy inside of you. As bright as a sun and let me tell you that it's just as lethal. If you misuse it or go farther than you are capable, you will wish that a little hexing was all you had to worry about."

She didn't have to say it. The implications were clear. Push too far, try for too much, and you will die. As I said, there was always a catch.

Calliope looked around the room with cursory eyes, studying each and every one of us. The room held their breath as if expecting her to continue her chastisement. However, she simply gave a wistful smile and closed her eyes briefly.

"Thankfully, none of you possess such a level to perform any of those kinds of magic." Her words made most of us sink in our seats. We were really the lowest of the bunch at Winchester Academy. We really couldn't expect to be able to do whatever kind of magic we wanted at the beginning.

Moving through the desks and back to the front, Calliope held up the bronze coin she had used on me earlier. "Before you are able to touch the stars, you must first be able to make the lowliest of magic. An energizer charm, the same in which I have used on

Miss Norman, is one of the most basic of the charms out there."

She swept her hand out across the room. "On the table in front of you, you will see a tray of coins just like this one. I want you to spend the rest of the class replicating the spell I used. If you don't finish today, it will also be your homework for next time." She paused in her speech and then her soft smile turned into a cruel smirk. "After all, you are the least of us and have a long way to go. Better to have a handful of these now, or you will surely fail." Her steel blue eyes locked onto me.

I tried not to let her look affect me as I worked on my charm, but I couldn't forget the message she had been clearly telling me. If I couldn't do this charm, I should give up. Even the weakest could do such a small charm.

But I'm not weak! I've already done many spells that were quite powerful. Of course, most of those weren't on purpose, but still ... Who is she to think I deserved such a look?

However, when the bell chimed that the end of class had come, I still hadn't cast the correct charm on the coin in front of me. I had one coin left. I had blown through the majority of the dozen she had given us to practice on already and all that was left of them were molten metal and ashy dust.

"Wow, you really suck at this."

My head jerked up from the table and met with Paul's brown eyes. I scrambled to throw away my failures and gather my things before he could see how horrible of a witch I really was.

"I'm still new," I muttered, keeping my eyes down. "I'll get it, eventually."

Paul chuckled and shook his head. "Not like that you won't."

My eyes filled with fire and shot up to meet his. "What's that supposed to me?"

Lifting his hands in front of him, Paul shook them slightly. "Woah, no need to get snappy. I'm just saying that, based on your failures, it seems like you lack focus."

My eyebrows raised. "I was focusing. I focused for almost an hour and only ended up with a bit pile of crap." I gestured wildly at the trash can.

Paul lifted a shoulder. "It takes more than just saying you are focusing. Magic isn't something you can just think about, and it happens."

I snorted. "It's always been that way before."

"But it wasn't the thought that did it, was it?" Paul asked, leaning a hand against the table. "You weren't really focusing on that thought. You were focusing … here." He touched his finger to where my heart sat beneath my chest.

His touch startled me enough that it took me a second to realize what he was saying. When he dropped his hand, I placed my own hand over my chest. "So, you're saying I'm thinking too much about and not feeling it?"

"Exactly." Paul grinned, causing that lickable dimple to show back up on his cheek. "It's not enough to want it in your head. You also have to want it in your heart. You have plenty of power, but if it doesn't have a direction, then that's what you'll get. A big pile of crap."

Hope swelled inside of me where there had been defeat and failure. So, I wasn't a bad witch after all.

As I sat through my next class, I thought about what Paul had said. Focusing with my mind wasn't enough. I wasn't putting any heart into it. I was just doing what I always did in school. I relied on my mind rather than my heart to get me through it. This wasn't high school or even a human school. I couldn't let myself think that I could do what I always did. I didn't know anything about being a witch so why would this be any different?

It was like I was trying to move a mountain with a bicycle. Brain power and drive wasn't going to be enough to get me where I needed to go. I had to prepare myself emotionally as well.

With my spirits lifted and a new determination in me, I made my way to lunch. There were only two more classes today and then I could work on making magic with my heart, not my mind.

"There you are!" an overly cheery voice cried out, and an arm looped through mine before I could react.

My head turned to find Sabrina latched onto my side with a smile on her face like we were best of friends. I didn't trust it.

"What do you want?" My body stiffened as she only smiled brighter.

"Can't I just want to say hi to one of my best friends?" Sabrina tilted her head slightly, giving me a confused look that most would find cute, but it only made my skin crawl.

I withdrew my arm from her and headed toward the lunch line, not even bothering to answer her.

"Oh, come on." Sabrina sighed, coming up behind me. "I'm not that bad once you get to know me. Really."

I couldn't help but snort-laugh. "Really? Because I was thinking you were less Sabrina the Teenage Witch and more Wicked Witch of the West." I smirked at her obvious distress.

"I am nothing of the sort." Sabrina flipped her hair over her shoulder with a huff. "We just got off on the wrong foot you mean. After all, if my Paul thinks you are worth talking to then obviously, I'm missing something."

Ah. That's it. Sabrina's only talking to me because she's threatened.

"So, can we start over or what?" Sabrina continued when I didn't respond. She picked up an apple and palmed it in her hands before taking a bottle of water as well.

That's all she's going to eat? I gaped at her and then looked down at my chili cheese fries. Compared to her I must look like some kind of enormous pig. Forcing back the sudden need to grab a salad, I grabbed a can of soda and a piece of chocolate cake just because. She would not make me feel bad about myself!

I scanned my card at the register and then turned to Sabrina. "I would be willing to start over." Sabrina opened her mouth, but I stopped her. "If you apologize."

Sabrina seemed taken back and then let out a groan of annoyance. "Fine, whatever.

Sorry, I made fun of you and your little friend. Are we good?"

Smiling tightly, I nodded.

"Good, then come eat with us." She grabbed my arm once more without warning and dragged me toward a table where Libby and Monica already sat.

My eye caught Trina a few tables over, and she made an obvious come-hither motion. I gestured my head toward Sabrina's table, and Trina gave me a confused look. I shrugged, not understanding it any more than she did. I'd have much rather sat with Trina that the trio before me, but I also didn't want to watch my back every second of the day.

"Hey, Max." Monica grinned, picking up her diet soda. Her plate only held a small salad. Did these girls not eat? Just looking at their lackluster plates made me want to die.

"Hey," I replied back and took a seat between Sabrina and Libby.

Libby smiled at me and then turned her eyes to Sabrina. "Did you hear? Lester Picarski and Rachel Boomtic were caught doing it in the potions lab this morning."

"No!" Sabrina gasped and then shook her head with a look of disgust. "I can't say I'm surprised. Rachel is as desperate as her

159

mother, and Lester will fuck anything that has a slit between their legs."

Libby and Monica giggled along with Sabrina, and I faked a chuckled. Picking at the food on my plate, I half-listened to them gossip about this student or that. Mostly they just picked apart people's outfits and talked crap about them. Then it was my turn.

"What about you, Max?" Libby asked, her eyes wide and blinking. "Is there a guy here you like?"

I swallowed the food in my mouth, almost choking on it. Quickly picking up my can of soda, I got the food lodged in my throat down and turned to their expectant faces. "Uh, no. Not really."

"Oh, come on." Monica smiled secretly. "You can tell us. We're your friends."

I eyeballed them and knew a trap when I saw one. "Uh, I've only been here a few days, I'd rather focus on getting caught up to everyone else's level than think about guys."

"Oh, so you like girls then?" Sabrina stated matter-of-factly.

"No, no. I'm not like that." I quickly answered, my face getting red.

"So defensive. Are you homophobic?" Sabrina continued her brows furrowed as if she actually believed it. "Libby, I'm sorry it seems Max hates lesbians. You can't be friends with her."

Libby frowned and started to stab her salad.

"I didn't say that!" I protested grabbing the edge of the table. "I don't hate lesbians. Lesbians are great. I think everyone should have more lesbian friends. We should all be lesbians. Really!" I didn't know what the hell I was saying, but I didn't want to get labeled as someone who hated others because of their sexual orientation. I didn't really. It wasn't any of my business who people loved.

"So, you *are* lesbian." Sabrina shot and then looked over my shoulder and said, "Sorry, Paul, looks like Max doesn't want your penis. So, shoo." She waved a hand in a shooing motion, and I slowly turned to see Paul standing behind me with a confused expression.

Turning back to the table, I buried my face in my hands. What the hell had just happened? I'd gotten stuck in a mean girl trap is what happened. I knew sitting with her was a bad idea. Why couldn't I have just said no and gone to sit with Trina instead?

"That's okay, Sabrina," Paul said, making me peek up from my hands. "I'm sure Max would still be a better girlfriend than you. At least, she wouldn't cheat on me."

161

Everyone at the table and around us stopped talking and stared at Paul. My eyes, however, were on Sabrina. Her face grew redder than the apple half-eaten on her plate. Then, all of a sudden, Sabrina stood to her feet and stomped out of the cafeteria. Her minions abandoned their food and ran after her, leaving me gaping at the table.

Paul sighed and then sat in Sabrina's abandoned seat. "Do you mind if I sit here? It seems anywhere else everyone will talk my ear off."

"No, no. Go for it." I nodded and turned back to my own tray.

After a few minutes of us silently eating our food, Paul glanced up at me. "So, to set the record straight, are you really not into guys?"

I giggled nervously. "Uh, yeah, about that …"

Chapter 12

SWEAT BEADED ON MY brow and my head started to ache, but I kept going. I could do this. I had to do this.

I stared at the bronze coin until my eyes crossed but still nothing. I sighed and leaned back in the chair I had claimed in the corner of the library. Rubbing my temple, I pulled my charms book closer to me and reread the passage Calliope had assigned us to study while we worked. Well, while those of us who couldn't charm their coin worked.

To cast a charm, one must focus their magical intent on the object. While bronze works best for charming at the beginning, other objects work as well as long as the intent is clear.

My intent was clear. My intent couldn't get any clearer even if it were made of crystal. What was I doing wrong?

"Still not getting it, huh?"

I glanced up from my book to see Paul leaning against the table with his arms folded over his broad chest. I couldn't help but let my eyes wander down his chest and to his long legs where he had his black boots crossed over the other. When they came back up his muscular form and met his bemused eyes, I blushed.

"So," - Paul flipped the pages of my book, his eyes scanning over the words - "Calliope is still spouting this crap."

"Crap?" I arched a brow.

Paul smirked. "Calliope is a great teacher, but she's not very good at breaking things down. She expects everyone to figure it out for themselves. She thinks anyone who can't isn't worth teaching."

I groaned in despair. "So, I'm doomed."

"Now, I wouldn't say that." Paul pulled out the chair next to me and sat down in it. "Okay, so show me what you're doing."

Glancing sideways at him, I hesitated. I wasn't getting anywhere on my own let alone with an audience. Though, having him watch might give me the extra incentive to get it right this time.

Scrounging up my courage, I took a deep breath and let it out. Turning my eyes back to the coin, I focused on that ball of light inside of me. I pulled at it, commanding it to move some of that energy into the bronze metal in front of me. It spiked for a moment or two, getting brighter, but then it settled once more as if it was too tired to be bothered.

I opened my eyes and sighed, not even looking at Paul to see what he thought.

"So ..." Paul smacked his lips. "You forgot everything I said before, didn't you?"

My head swiveled in his direction. "No, I didn't. I'm doing like you said. Focusing my emotions on putting the magic into the coin."

Paul chuckled dryly. "Well, if that is what you call emotion, I feel bad for your boyfriend."

I licked my lips and shifted in my seat. "I don't have a boyfriend."

"Ah, it all makes sense."

My eyes widened, and I scowled. "What's that supposed to mean?"

"Have you ever had a boyfriend?" Paul asked, his expression not taunting but full of interest. "Or someone you liked a lot?"

I shifted even more in my seat. "I've dated. I had a long-term relationship up until the end of high school."

"What happened?"

Hesitating to answer, I watched Paul's face. I couldn't tell if he was asking because he wanted to know or if it was still part of the lesson. Either way, I wasn't getting anywhere staring at the coin. If the only way I was going to figure out how to finish my assignment was to give up a bit of personal information, then I guess I could play ball.

Turning my face away from him, I stared down at the coin. "It didn't work out."

"Oh please, stop. You are a fountain of information." Paul held his hands up and leaned back in his chair, the sarcasm in his voice not amusing.

My shoulders sagged. "What do you want me to say? He was my first real boyfriend. We dated. I thought I loved him and he loved me. Then out of the blue, he wants to break up. We were both going to college on opposite sides of the country and as he said, 'Long-distance relationships are too hard.'"

Paul was quiet for a moment and then placed his hand on top of mine. "I'm sorry that happened to you. That's a shit way to get dumped. Especially by someone you really cared about."

I offered him a weak smile, trying to force back all my feelings of Jaron. "Thanks." Clearing my throat, I moved my chair closer to the table. "So, not that talking about my love life isn't fun, but was there a point to all this?"

Giving me that dimple-peeking grin, Paul leaned his face on his arm. "Can't I just want to know about you? Weighing what kind of guy I'm up against?"

I threw my head back and laughed. "You are a charming one, aren't you? But rest assured there's no competition. Jaron made it clear where we stood."

The image of Jaron's robe catching on fire filled my head. I'd wanted for him to hurt. To know how much it had burned me for him to drop me so easily. I'd thought he loved me. He'd told me he loved me.

"I feel there is more to that story, but I'll let it go." He winked at me. "For now." Moving off his arm, he picked up the coin and placed it in my hand. My skin warmed where he touched me. "But I have to admit I do have an ulterior motive for asking. You see, that emotion you were feeling just now?" Paul brushed my hair away from my face as I tried to hide. "That emotion is what will make or break your spells." He brushed his thumb against the curve of my cheek, making my heart jump in my chest.

"See, people think magic is all about some fancy words or a piece of wood focusing the energy, but really it's the emotion. That's what makes us magical. That's what gives our intentions life. Use that emotion, Max. Feel."

He leaned forward until our nose brushed against one another and my breath caught in my throat. Just for a second, I almost leaned into him. Almost let our mouth meet, but then the coin in my hand warmed and then burned hot enough that I had to drop it.

"Crap." I shoved my chair back and bent down to pick up the coin. Paul moved back to his seat while I tested the coin to see if it was still hot. Surprisingly, it was cool to the touch now. Frowning, I put the coin on the table. "Does it always happen like that?"

Instead of Paul answering, it was another voice. "Only when the emotion is higher than normal. Plus, where the power is coming from helps."

I jumped in place and spun around to see Ian standing by the bookshelf hiding my little nook. "Uh, how long have you been there for?"

"Long enough." Ian smirked that sexy smirk of his making me feel things I really shouldn't have after almost having kissed Paul just a few moments ago. "So, I see you're playing the dutiful tutor as always Paul." Ian nodded his head toward the quiet male. I didn't like Ian's implications of Paul.

What was he saying? Did Paul always hit on girls this way?

"It's not like that, Ian." There was a bit of a bite in Paul's words, and I glanced between the two of them. There was something similar about them. I mean, not right this instant. Since Paul was glaring at Ian and Ian didn't seem to have a care in the world, but there was something. Something I couldn't put my finger on.

"Well, it is your usual MO, isn't it?" Ian sauntered over to us and placed himself between Paul and me. "Find a pretty girl, chat her up, tell her it's all about the emotion and then boom. You make your move."

Mortification started to billow inside of me as I glanced at Paul, begging him to deny it. Paul avoided my gaze and kept shooting daggers at Ian with his eyes. Gritting my teeth, I couldn't believe how stupid I'd been. Of course, a guy like that would have tons of girls, I wasn't anything special.

"Why do you have to be such a dick?" Paul stood to his feet and moved into Ian's personal space.

"Why do you have to be so predictable?" Ian shifted so that they were nose-to-nose. If there hadn't been such a thick amount of animosity in the air, I'd have thought they were going to kiss just like Paul and I had almost done. Boy, was I glad that hadn't happened now.

"And what?" Paul sniffed. "I'm supposed to just pop up everywhere they go and pretend like I was already there and not purposely trying to run into them like you do?" Paul shoved a finger into Ian's chest. "Stalkerish much?"

"Hey, you have your ways, and I have mine." Ian shoved Paul away slightly and then grinned. "My ways just happen to make me look cool and take way less effort than trying to figure out whatever homework they need help on."

"At least, I'm taking an interest in what she's doing. That's more than I can say for you, who only cares about what's in her pants and not her brains."

Ian snorted. "So little you know about me, little brother."

That was the last straw. They were arguing over me as if I weren't even here. And Ian's comment about being his brother? What the hell was up with that?

"Does someone want to tell me what's going on?" I growled, my anger starting to fester inside of me. I'd been nothing but nice to Paul and everyone else I had met here at the academy, save Sabrina who had been nasty first. Why they thought it was okay to

170

play games with me, I didn't know. Maybe it was some kind of wizard thing.

"What's going on, sweet little Maxine," - Ian turned his eyes from Paul for a moment to look at me - "is that little brother doesn't know how to change up his game. Especially when dealing with someone out of his league." His hazel eyes scanned up and down my form. I felt like a lamb about to be gobbled up by the wolf, but I had a feeling I wouldn't mind it one bit. This only made me even more irritated.

The books on the tables and shelves around us started to shake in place. The pen next to my notebook rolled off the table and on to the floor, landing with a loud clack. Paul and Ian stopped their testosterone-filled staring contest to gape at me.

"Max," Paul said slowly as if I were a skittish deer he was afraid would bolt at any moment. "Remember what I said about your emotions controlling your magic? Well, that also goes for when you don't want it to."

I scoffed. "Who said I don't want to? You're the ones acting so high and mighty. So, what if I didn't grow up learning about magic? So, what if I'm a bit behind? But at least, I'm a decent human being who doesn't go around playing games with people just to get their kicks."

"You tell him, sister," Ian added.

My volatile gaze turned on him. "Don't talk to me as if you didn't have a hand in this. You've been skulking around me from the beginning. How do I know you and your *brother*," I spat, "don't do this all the time? Find a sweet little first year and mess with her head? Huh? Or maybe this is some sick game Sabrina cooked up?" I searched around for that big blonde head of hers, but to my dissatisfaction, it was nowhere to be found.

"What's that she-bitch got to do with this?" Ian frowned, his brows furrowing together in confusion.

"Well, she is Paul's ex-girlfriend." My lips spread wide as I smiled at Paul and then turned my attention back to Ian. "And from what I hear, she cheated on him with you, his brother?" I raised my brows and laughed at the hilarity of it. "Man, and I thought my life was fucked up." I shook my head, and then all of a sudden, the anger I had to destroy the very ground beneath us was gone, and I sighed all that emotion out. Looking between the two of them as I packed up my bags, I clucked my tongue. "You really should work on your family issues before trying to get into it over another girl because really," - I slammed Ian on the shoulder as I walked by - "I'd have given anything for a sibling growing up, so you best make nice with the one you've got."

I started to walk away from the two of them, tired of all these games and just wanting to get a good night's sleep. However, fate was not so kind. When I was mid-library, in the heart of the majority of its occupants, a hand clamped down on my shoulder and turned me.

Ian stood there with a wicked grin on his lips and my pen in his hand. "You forgot this, Mancaster."

A round of gasps and whispers scattered throughout the library. I glanced around to see all the eyes on us, and several people texting away on their phones, no doubt telling everyone they know what they'd heard. So much for keeping it quiet.

"I should have made Dale memory wipe you too," I growled, taking the pen from him with more force than necessary.

Ian ran a hand through his hair and smiled. "He might be able to take care of a few lower beings, but I'm on a whole other level, baby."

"I'm not your baby," I snapped and then added, "And it's Norman. Not Mancaster. Get it right." I stomped away from him and toward the door, his laughter chasing after me.

"Whatever you say, Mancaster," Ian called out after me, making me grit my teeth even harder.

As I rushed down the hallway and back toward my room, I could feel all the eyes on me. It was like they were undressing me with their eyes and seeing down to my very being. I didn't like it one bit.

In my rush to get to my room, I didn't pay close enough attention to where I was going and once more ran straight into someone. Falling flat on my butt, I winced.

"I'm sorry, I wasn't watching where I was going," I apologized as I scrambled to get up. A large hand took my arm and lifted me up from the ground and onto my feet. My eyes lifted to Aidan's captivating blue eyes.

"Are you okay?"

I was startled by his question. More so because he barely seemed to talk to me at all and not by the fact that his voice did naughty things to my insides.

I moved my head up and down quickly and pulled my things closer to me. "I'm okay. Thanks. Sorry again. You know, for running you over."

Aidan coughed strangely. Was he laughing?

174

"Is something funny?" I asked, my irritation from earlier rearing back full force. The guys at this school really were trying to get on my shit list.

"The thought of a tiny thing like you running me over is funny." His words wrapped around me and settled down low, tightening things.

My annoyance disappeared, and I shifted in place. "Well, I pack a powerful punch. Just ask the Broomstein brothers." I pointed my thumb back toward the library.

Aidan made that coughing laugh noise again. "They are dumb boys. Always fighting over what the other has."

"Really?"

"Don't let them put you in the middle." Aidan's eyes turned serious and settled on me. "You are worth more than that."

A bit dumbfounded, I could only nod with my mouth gaping open like a fish. Aidan seemed to take that answer as acceptable and went on his way. As I continued the rest of the way to my dorm room, I realized something. I liked Aidan. He might be quiet and intimidating as all get out, but he didn't seem the type to ever lie to me. Or play games. I needed more people like that in my life. It didn't hurt that just looking at him made my mouth water.

175

"Oh, my Merlin," Trina cried out the moment I stepped into our room. She rushed at me with her phone in her hand, and I could only stifle a groan. "When were you going to tell me you're one of *the* Mancasters? Here I've been hanging my dirty clothes all over the place, and you're like magical royalty."

I shook my head and pushed past her, leaving my bag on the floor by the bed as I collapsed on it. "That's my grandparents, not me."

"Well, it's you now," Trina continued even though I couldn't see her. "It's all over the school. They are saying the Broomstein brothers have found another gold star to fight over. You know, it was Sabrina last year, but now it's you! Aren't you excited?" She practically squealed like a fangirl seeing her favorite movie star.

I sighed and rolled over. "Yeah, thrilled."

Chapter 13

BREATHE IN THROUGH THE nose. Sigh it out. Arms up in the air, then fold down to forward fold. Rinse and repeat.

The fact that I hadn't done any of my stretches the last few days showed how out of place I'd felt here at Winchester Academy. I used to do them every morning and every night like clockwork. This would be the first morning I'd done them since arriving. My mom would tear me a new one if she knew I'd been so lax, especially when I needed to center myself the most.

"Does that stuff really work?"

"Sometimes." I shrugged a shoulder while still upside down and glanced to where Trina sat on her bed, a book in her lap and her notebook and pen floating in the air as they took notes. It was times like these that I wished I was able to do the kind of magic she could. I'd only been at the academy for a few days, and already I was getting antsy to do something bigger.

And the earthquake I caused in the library wasn't big enough?

Okay, so not bigger stuff. I had the big stuff down. More like the non-destructive stuff side. I let out a sigh that had nothing to do with my stretches and stood up.

"You know," Trina put her book to the side, and her pen stopped taking notes. "I don't understand what the big deal is. So, your grandparents are some hot shots in the magical community." She shrugged as if it were no big deal. "I'd be thrilled. Think of all the benefits you'd get from their name alone."

"Like what?" I moved my feet into a modified version of warrior one. "So, I can be friends with people like Sabrina?" I rolled my eyes and then tried to focus on my breathing. The ball of light in my head burned brightly and more vibrantly the longer I stayed in the pose. I released the position, and the energy dissipated as well.

"No," Trina drew out, her nose scrunched up as if the thought of hanging out with Sabrina was the last thing she wanted to do. I didn't blame her. "But you could get into all the cool parties! Plus, I hear the privileged hall has way better rooms, and you can use the cafeteria whenever you want. Even have a car on campus as a first year." I could see the stars in Trina's eyes at all the possibilities my family name came with.

Sitting down on my pad cross-legged, I pointed a finger at her. "You forget, all that comes with strings attached. I don't want to start using my grandparent's name and then have them show up one day, demanding I fall in line." I straightened my back and lifted my chin. "I'm my own woman after all."

Trina giggled just as my phone beeped.

Callie: How's it going? Touch anybody's wand yet?

I snort-laughed out loud at Callie's text.

"What is it?" Trina moved off the bed to sit beside me on the ground. I started to show her Callie's text but then hesitated. Then I shook my head. She couldn't possibly know that Callie was a human just from a text message. I handed her the phone.

Trina's brow scrunched together. "She does know wands are so cliché, right? No one uses wands. At least, no one cool."

I raised a brow at Trina's matter-of-fact statement. "I don't think that's what she meant."

It took her a second before her eyes widened and her mouth dropped open. "OH!"

179

She paused for a second and then asked, "So have you?"

I groaned. I needed to get myself some non-perverted friends.

Seeming to take my groan as an answer, Trina changed the subject. "So, who's Callie? Someone from your pre-witch life?"

I stiffened at her question. Could I trust Trina, or would she hold it against me like I felt like Dale was doing? I mean, he didn't blab but maybe she would. Then again, Trina was my roommate. It was going to be hard to keep secrets from her. I was not the best of liars.

"Can you keep a secret?" I asked after a long moment.

Trina's eyes brightened and shifted closer, a bit more eager than I'd expected she'd be. "Of course! What kind of roommate or friend would I be if I didn't keep your secrets?"

I chewed on my lower lip for a moment still not a hundred percent sure I should tell her but then finally gave in. "So, I have this best friend from high school. Her name's Callie. And I sort of—"

"Told her you're a witch?" Trina finished for me, her shoulders sagging with disappointment.

"Uh, yeah." I slowly said watching her face closely.

"Pfft." Trina waved me off. "You think you're the only one who's broken that rule? And here I thought it was something really good."

I shifted so that I could face her directly. "What do you mean? I thought it was like the number one rule?"

Trina shrugged. "Well, it is, but do you really think the council is going to hunt down every single person who knows about us? They'd be wiping memories twenty-four seven."

"Really?" I relaxed a bit. And here I thought I was doing the most taboo of rule breaking. "They really wipe people's memories?"

"Sure, if they end up being a problem. You have to be licensed for it because playing with someone's mind is big magic."

I thought back to when Dale had erased the memories of the students in line the other day. He hadn't done much of anything before they were back to not knowing who I was.

"What about here at the school?"

Trina barked a laugh. "Oh, yeah, you better believe it. All the professors and workers are licensed to do memory alterations. Even some of the student assistants."

"Why?"

"To keep the school's image of course and if any humans randomly come on to grounds at the same time someone is doing magic." Trina smacked her hands on her legs and stood up. "That's why we aren't allowed to do magic out of our bedrooms or classrooms. Oh, and the library, but you already knew that." She winked at me before gathering her books for today's classes.

Note to self: word travels fast in Winchester Academy.

I grabbed my bag and followed Trina out the door. I'd already eaten a granola bar in my room so I wouldn't have to go to the cafeteria for breakfast. Just imagining all the stares I would get made me shudder. I wasn't ready to face that yet. At least in the hallway, I could keep moving and wasn't stuck in one place. It would be bad enough when I was sitting in class. I just hoped a certain someone hadn't heard about it yet.

"Hey, Norman!"

My shoulder shot up to my ears, and I winced. I contemplated pretending like I hadn't heard my name shouted by the very person I wanted to avoid, but it was no use. Sabrina was on me like warts on a toad.

"That is your name, right?" Sabrina asked, her brows raised as she crossed her arms over her low-neck halter top. "Because I heard a rumor going around that you aren't exactly who you say you are. That's not true, right? We're friends. Friends don't lie to each other."

"Yeah, friends don't lie," Libby said from behind me causing me to jump and turn around slightly. Libby and Monica stood at my back with Sabrina attacking me from the front. I was surrounded by Witch Barbies.

"I didn't lie," I claimed, holding my bag's strap tighter. I didn't bother correcting them about being friends. One drama at a time was all I could take.

"So, then it's not true?" A slow, triumphant smile started to crawl up Sabrina's face, and I couldn't help but want to squash it.

Cocking my head to the side, I asked with a slight grin, "Well, that depends on what you are referring to. Is it that I shook the whole library? Or that the Broomstein brothers were fighting over me? You really have to be more specific."

Sabrina's face reddened considerably, her hands tightening on her arms as if trying to keep herself from attacking me. "I'm talking about the fact that you are masquerading as a bottom feeder when you are clearly a Mancaster. I don't know how I didn't see it before. You have that 'rules don't apply to me' mentality they all have." She sniffed and flipped her hair over her shoulder. "Hardly worthy of the title of wizarding royalty. Really, it's wasted on the likes of you."

I pretended to pout. "Oh, but I thought we were friends?"

"We are friends," Monica said from behind me. "Aren't we?"

A wicked grin covered Sabrina's obvious annoyance with me. "Yeah, Monica. You're right, we are friends. So, let me give you a little piece of advice." Sabrina leaned forward and placed her hand on my shoulder. I glanced at it like it was an unwanted fly. "You might be a Mancaster, but you're still a human-bred bottom feeder, and bottom feeders don't get guys like Paul and Ian." Her fingernails bit into my shoulder as she gnashed her teeth. "If you were wise, you'd steer clear of them." The 'or else' was implied as Sabrina's face smoothed over a cute smile took over. "Alright, friend?"

She didn't give me the chance to answer before she engulfed me in a hug that made all my hairs stand on end. As soon as it started, it was over, and Sabrina and her minions were sauntering down the hallway, barking at people as they went.

"A real piece of work that one is." Ian's voice came from my left. "What a waste." Tsking, he took a bite out of the apple in his hand. Against my will, my eyes were drawn to his lips, and I forced myself to look away.

Snorting, I moved toward my first class of the day. "You slept with her."

"Hold your tongue." Ian followed after me without permission. "I did no such thing."

Waiting at the door of Professor Piston's class, I raised a brow at Ian. "That's not what she thinks or your brother."

Ian leaned one arm against the wall and lowered his head slightly down to my level. "And do you believe everything you hear?"

I huffed. "Whether or not it's true is beside the point. I'm still mad at you for letting out my secret."

Placing a hand on his heart, Ian pouted. "You wound me. I have it under good authority that you would have been ousted quite soon by the she-bitch very soon."

"How's that?" I sighed, impatient for the conversation to be over.

"Because I know things like that." Ian took another bite of his apple and grinned. It really wasn't fair for him to look that good. Him or his brother. Their parents must have used some kind of sorcery to make them that perfect.

They're not perfect. They're jackasses using you for their petty game.

"Whatever." I turned away from him to enter the class, but he grabbed my arm pulling me back to his side.

"Now, now. I'm not done. Don't you want to know how I know?"

"Not particularly."

"Well, then I'm not going to tell you about the bag of secrets that she-bitch has been collecting since she could talk." Ian tried to bait me, but unfortunately, this fish had no interest in biting.

"Goodbye, Ian." I tried once again to go to class, but this time Ian jumped in front of the door. "Let me by."

Holding his hands up in front of him, Ian's expression changed to that of a contrite puppy for tearing up my favorite shoes. "Look, can we start over? I'm sorry I gave you the wrong impression. I really wasn't planning on fighting over you with my brother."

"Oh, really?" I pursed my lips, not believing him for a second.

"Believe it. I just saw a cute girl at the store and a chance to get to know her. That's all." He held his hands out as if to show me he had no tricks up his sleeves.

"So, it was just a coincidence your brother hit on me the moment I stepped on campus?" I hummed. I wasn't born yesterday. It was obvious they had some kind of family drama going on, and I didn't want to be any part of it.

Lifting a shoulder, Ian smirked. "What can I say? We have good taste."

I scoffed and tried to push past him, but he wouldn't budge. "You think you're such a smooth talker, don't you?"

Ian puffed up his chest, not at all ashamed. "I like to think I'm charming."

Rolling my eyes, I let out an exasperated sigh. "What will it take to get you to let me by?"

"How about a date?"

I turned on my heel only to run into another Broomstein brother. Glaring up at a curious Paul, I'd had enough. "What the hell? Can't I just go to class and be left alone in peace! I don't want to be friends with Miss Queen Witch or get stuck in some testosterone tug of war. I just want to learn magic and get on with my life."

"I couldn't have said it better myself."

All three of us turned to where Professor Piston stood behind Ian with a rather perturbed expression on his face. Ian quickly moved out of the doorway allowing the professor to come through. Piston's eyes moved between the three of us, and he took his glasses off for a moment to clean the lens.

"I don't know what the complete circumstances are, but from Miss Norman's outburst, I've gotten the gist." Putting his glasses back on his nose, he shot a stern look at Ian. "Your family name may allow you to do a lot of things, but disrupting my classroom is not one of them. I suggest you take yourself back to where you belong. In the basement."

Ian scowled at Piston. He glanced my way one more time, his eyes clearly telling me this wasn't over before heading back down the hallway.

"As for you," Piston's eyes moved to Paul. "I am appalled to hear one of my favorite students has nothing better to do than play with a young girl's emotions. Shame on you."

Paul ducked his head, a thoroughly dejected look on his face. "My apologies, Professor. I have no excuses."

Piston sniffed. "As you shouldn't." When those hard eyes landed on me, I stiffened. "As for you, Miss Norman. Or would you prefer Mancaster?"

"Norman, please," I said in a small voice afraid to even speak.

"Very well. You should have more pride in yourself as a person and as a witch. As you said, you are here to learn magic, not get a physical education." Piston's eyes shot to Paul for a moment. "I would hate to see you not reach your potential because you were distracted by unnecessary drama. I'm sure your parents and grandparents would agree, don't you?"

Licking my lips, I shook my head. "I don't know what my grandparents would think since I haven't even met them."

Piston gave me a smile, and it wasn't a nice one. "I wouldn't expect that to be that way for long. From my experience with your family, the Mancasters are never the type to let their young ones run wild. Plan for a visit from them sooner if not later." With those words, Piston marched back into his classroom followed by Paul who never even looked my way.

Taking a few deep cleansing breaths, I entered as well. I wasn't sure if what Piston had said was true, but I couldn't take the chance of him being right. If my grandparents thought they were going to control me the way they tried to control mom, they had another thing coming.

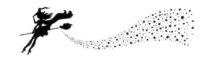

Chapter 14

"HOW'S IT GOING?" TRINA asked, dropping into the chair next to me in the library. "We still up for shopping today?"

I glanced up from my book and rubbed my eyes. "Yeah, I need a break. My brain's about to turn into mush, which is less than I can say for this assignment."

The big reveal of me being a Mancaster blew over way faster than expected. I still got a few stares every once in a while, but once everyone heard that I wanted to go by Norman, they all seemed to relax. After that, everything turned back to normal. The weeks went by in a blur. I went to class, I had lunch, sometimes I hung out with Callie afterward, but soon she had to go to Brown, and it was just me against Winchester Academy.

Thankfully, Sabrina seemed to have lost interest in me or was biding her time. Either way, I was back to hanging out with Trina.

Sometimes Dale would sit with us at lunch, but for the most part, I was just us two. Dale still hadn't mentioned Callie, and I was too chicken to bring it up. However, if what Trina said was true, then I shouldn't have any reason to worry.

"It can't be that hard of a spell." Trina looked down at the rock in front of me on the table. I'd finally gotten to move up to a more advanced class. Apparently, the basics only took a month when you had Mancaster blood working the mojo. Another aspect that had people talking and staring.

"Then you take a whack at it." I shoved the rock toward her. "I'm supposed to turn this rock into a cup."

Trina picked up the rock and turned it over in her hands. "What kind of cup?"

I shrugged and leaned on my arm. "I don't know, just a cup. Any kind of cup."

Shaking her head, Trina handed me the rock back. "Well, that's your problem. You can't just say any old cup. You have to be specific. Is it plastic? Metal? What color is it? Imagine yourself drinking from it, how would it feel? Those kinds of things."

Frowning, I took the rock back and sat it on the table. The Transfiguration professor hadn't told us what kind of cup. He had said visualize it in your mind and make it happen.

I'd been visualizing for a good thirty minute and have gotten squat. However, now that Trina mentioned it, my image of a cup was more of a blur than a cup.

I took a deep breath and closed my eyes, bringing a cup to mind. My favorite mug from home. It was large and rounded with a purple base and white polka dots. I remembered what it felt like to have the cup in my hand full of hot chocolate with those tiny marshmallows piled so high they hardly fit the mug.

"Woah."

Trina's exclamation had my eyes popping open. My rock had turned into my mug from home alright, but it had also come along with the hot chocolate and marshmallows too. Well, that was one way of doing it.

I picked the mug up and brought it to my nose. Inhaling deeply, the sweet chocolaty liquid warmed my insides. Glancing at Trina, I asked, "Think it's safe to drink?"

Lifting a shoulder, she shook her head. "I don't see why not."

The mug touched my lips, and I took a hesitant sip. Immediately, I sat back in my chair and let out a moan of pleasure. It tasted exactly like the kind my dad made me with milk and everything.

"Good?"

Grinning, I took another drink. "So good."

Trina grinned back and then started to study me. "You know, that was some serious spell work just now. You couldn't even work the spell at first, and then next thing you know, you are producing something out of nothing."

Reluctantly sitting the cup down, I watched her. "Is that a bad thing? I mean, I'm not pretending to be bad at magic or anything to show off."

"Oh, I know you aren't. I've watched you take notes. Freaking OCD central." Trina laughed. "But others might think so. I, however, think you are just a natural which would make sense because of your family."

I scowled. I hated when people referenced my family as the reason I got something or was able to do something. I wanted them to say I was good because of me not because of some family I never knew.

"Sorry." Trina touched my arm, having seen my expression. "I didn't mean it like that."

Giving her a bitter smile, I nodded. "I know. It's just frustrating. I work so hard to do this on my own, and my family name still gets credit."

All of a sudden Trina stood to her feet. "You know what this calls for?"

193

"What?"

"Shopping!" she grabbed my arm, forcing me to stand. "Come on. You've been doing this crap long enough. It's time for some retail therapy."

I snorted. "You sound just like Callie." Man, did I miss that girl. We'd been in constant contact since she left, but it wasn't the same. I missed her face. And video chats weren't the same. I needed my best friend.

You did this to yourself.

"Well, Callie is my kind of girl, and I can't wait to meet her." Trina threw her arm over my shoulder her hair bouncing into my head. "Now, let's get going. The Halloween Mixer is not too much further off, and we still haven't gotten anything to wear."

Groaning at the reminder, I gathered my books and put them in my bag. "Don't remind me."

"What? Don't you like parties?" Trina picked up the mug and took a drink from it, smacking her lips. "Man, that is good."

"Told you." I grinned and then focused on turning the mug back into a rock. It changed right at Trina put it to her lips making it look like she was kissing it. Laughing at her, I dodge her arm swinging to hit me.

"That's not funny. I could have chipped a tooth." She grumbled, crossing her arms over her chest.

"Nah, I wouldn't let you do that."

We left the library and stopped by our room so I could drop my bag off before heading toward the bus stop. Unfortunately, I didn't have a car, Mancaster or not, so I couldn't take advantage of that perk that Trina constantly whined about.

"Where do you want to go first?" I asked once we were seated on the bus. "I mean, what do you even wear to a Halloween mixer? A dress? A costume?"

Trina tapped her chin in thought. "Well, I guess we can forgo the usual robes and pointed hats since we're in college now. Though I wouldn't advise showing up in some kind of costume unless you want to get the stink eye." She stared at me so seriously that I believed her for a second. Until she burst out laughing, pointing a finger at my face. "I'm joking, but your face really. Priceless."

"Jerk." I nudged her with my elbow.

"Consider it payback for the rock." Trina sniffed, putting her nose in the air.

Holding my hands up, I chuckled. "Consider me thoroughly paid back."

Relaxing in her seat, Trina pulled out her phone. "In any case, you can wear whatever you want, really. It doesn't say on the school site that there's a dress code. I plan on looking hot!" She bounced in her seat, her phone clutched tightly in her hands. "Just wait until they get a look at me. They will be lining up to dance with this sweet ass."

Giggling at her face, I raised a curious brow. "Any person in particular or just everyone in general?"

As the bus stopped, Trina blushed. "No, not really."

I followed after her as we got off the bus at the mall. "Really? It's going to be like that? I tell you all about my secrets, ones that will get me in trouble and you won't even tell me who you like? I see how it is." I sniffed and pretended to be offended.

"It's not like that." Trina hurried to explain. "It's not that don't want to tell you. It's just embarrassing."

"How could whoever you like be embarrassing? If you like them, then they can't be anything but wonderful." I looped my arm with hers and led her to the first dress store.

We looked through the racks for a few minutes before Trina finally broke the silence. "It's Libby Moreling."

"What's Libby Moreling?" I asked, holding up a black dress that was cut a bit too low for my taste. I held it up to Trina who shook her head, so I put it back.

"Libby is the person I like."

I didn't say anything for a moment.

"See?" Trina pointed a finger at me. "I knew you'd react this way. She's not as bad as she seems. Really!"

I shook my head. "I'm not questioning your choice of person, really. I'm just stunned. Libby always seemed so ..." I tried to find a nice word for how I felt about the glazed-eyed blonde with the large chest.

"I know, I know." Trina picked up a bright pink dress with lace all over and held it out. When I shook my head, she put it back with a loud clank. "She seems really simple-minded, but she's actually really nice."

I quirked a brow.

"When she's not around Sabrina," Trina explained. "I have Stars and Signs with her, and she's actually quite bright. People just think she's dumb because she doesn't share her opinion much."

"I wonder why?" I snorted. With friends like Sabrina, I'd be afraid to say anything too out of character as well. I picked up a pale blue dress made of silky material. The front had a neckline that would give me cleavage but not enough to flash the room, and the straps started as one and then into two as it went around to the back where the four straps crisscrossed. I knew if I put it on it would fall about to my mid-thigh which was sexy, yet I wasn't showing the world my underwear.

"Oo, I like that one. You should totally get it." Trina fingered the dress with clear appreciation in her eyes.

"I like it too. So, what about you? Find anything?" I glanced at her hands to see them empty and frowned.

"No, not yet, but the day is young!" Trina grinned.

I went to the counter to check out. After I was done, I let Trina take me into several other stores until she found the perfect dress, a red off the shoulder dress that hugged her hips and swirled around her legs. If she didn't grab attention at the mixer, then I had no hope for the future magical community.

"Do you really like it?" Trina asked for the millionth time while we were sitting in the food court eating lunch.

"Yes, it's great. Libby will love it. I'm sure." I popped a fry in my mouth as I watched the people pass by. This had been exactly what I needed. I loved the magic at school, but sometimes I just wanted to feel like a normal girl again. Today had definitely done that.

My eye caught onto someone sitting a few tables down from us. "It's that Monica?"

"Where?" Trina sat up in her chair straighter her eyes going to where I was looking. "Yeah, that's her. Do you think Libby's with her?" Her eyes scanned the food court searching for her crush.

I pursed my lips. "I'd be more worried about Sabrina being with here than Libby. In any case, it looks like she's alone." I watched Monica for a moment.

Her eyes were down on the table, and her brows were drawn in. She had food on a tray before her. A cheeseburger and fries, something I would never see her eat at school.

"She seems upset," I said and then stood up. "I'm going to go talk to her."

"Wait," Trina called out to me. "What if she's not alone?"

I didn't stop but did turn slightly back to her with a wink. "Then at least, I have back-up." Trina frowned but didn't protest anymore.

Walking over to where Monica sat, I kept my eyes out for any unseen witches. Wouldn't want to get in a fight in the middle of the mall and have the council down on our heads. Thankfully, when I arrived at her table, there was no sign of Sabrina or any other students from the school.

"Hey, Monica." This close up I could see the tears that she was fighting to let free, her eyes glistening and her nose a bit red.

Her eyes jerked up from the table at my greeting, and she quickly wiped her eyes and nose, sitting up straighter in her seat. "Oh, hi, Max. What's up?"

I pointed a thumb at Trina. "Just doing some shopping for the Halloween Mixer. What about you?"

"Oh, you know," she started, and I could clearly see her struggling for an excuse. "Just ruining my life." I startled at her sudden honesty as she burst into tears.

Glancing at the crying girl and then back to Trina who only shrugged. Turning back to Monica, I patted her on the shoulder. "It's okay. I'm sure it's not that bad. Nothing you can't fix right?"

Monica sat up and sniffed, hiccupping as she tried to speak. "If I want to lose all my friends and put a target on my back, then sure."

My brow furrowed for a moment and then it clicked. "This has to do with Sabrina, doesn't it?"

Nodding, Monica used a napkin to wipe her nose. "People thinks she's this great person," - I forced myself not to snort - "but really, she can be a vicious bitch, especially when it comes to Paul."

This time my eyebrows raised to my hairline. "This has to do with Paul. Do you like him?" A small part of me that I couldn't understand ached. It hoped she'd say no. It was stupid because I didn't like Paul or Ian. They could both go blow themselves up for all I care. At least, that's what I told myself.

"No, it's nothing like that," Monica said and then huffed. "Okay, so you know I'm majoring in Herbs and Medicines, right?"

No, I didn't, but I nodded anyway.

"Well, I really wanted to major in Potions."

My eyes squinted as I tried to figure out what that had to do with anything. "Then why don't you?"

Monica's voice rose an octave. "Because Paul majors in Potions. If I got anywhere near him, Sabrina would throw me to the curb like yesterday's toadstool."

"But you don't like Paul," I said, still not getting it.

"Exactly!"

I pursed my lips and sat back in my chair. Sabrina was worse than I thought. Not only does she bully the lower classes and anyone who looked at Paul, but she bullied her own friends. Libby - sorry, Trina - didn't seem to have enough rocks in her head to even notice she was being bullied, but clearly, Monica was the smarter of the three. I didn't understand why she even went along with it.

"So, you're upset because you are doing a major that you don't really want to do because if you did the one you wanted to do, you would lose your friend and would thus be ostracized?" I recapped what she had said to me to make sure I had it right.

"Yes."

"So, did Sabrina specifically say you couldn't major in Potions?" I asked, trying to work out a solution.

Monica paused in wiping her nose. "Well, no. She didn't, but I know that she didn't like anyone near Paul. If Libby or I even looked his way for longer than necessary, she would have a bitch fit."

"Okay," I drew out. "But aren't you a first year?"

"Yeah, so?"

"And Paul's, what, a third year?"

"Yeah, I think so." Monica tilted her head to the side.

"Then why do you think you would even have any classes with him? In fact, you could always make sure your classes were different dates and times than his. Then it would solve the whole problem."

Monica was quiet for a moment as if having a hard time to process my words. Then her mouth spread wide into the happiest grin I'd ever seen. She jumped up from her seat and hugged me tightly. I patted her back a bit awkwardly.

"Thank you so much. I can't believe I hadn't thought of that." Monica pulled back from me. "You are such a lifesaver, really."

I waved her off. "Oh, it was nothing. Just happy to help." I started to head back to my table, but she stopped me.

"You know, I'm not supposed to tell you," Monica started, her eyes darting around her. "But I heard that Paul was working up the courage to ask you to the mixer. Ian too."

"Why can't you tell me?"

Chewing on her lower lip, Monica lowered her voice. "Because Sabrina will flip if she finds out he chose you over her."

"Well, Sabrina doesn't have to worry. I have no interest in either Broomstein brother." I grinned at her, but as I was heading back to my table, my heart was beating a mile a minute.

I was such a big fat liar.

Chapter 15

A FEW DAYS LATER, I sat in the courtyard eating my lunch and reading my Potions book. Usually, I ate inside the cafeteria, but today I was behind on work, and the cafeteria had too many distractions. At least out here, there were fewer people, most of them doing exactly the same as me. So, it was no surprise when I became so absorbed in my own work I didn't realize anyone was near me until a shadow covered the page I was reading.

"Hey!" I cried out, jerking my head up from my book. "Do you mind?"

A reddish-brown mop of hair blocked out most of the sun, and a frown marred Dale's face. Once he noticed what I was mad about, he quickly moved out of the way and sat beside me. "Sorry."

"It's fine. I needed a break anyway," I muttered, putting a bookmark in my place and sitting in on the ground. "So, what's up?"

Dale seemed a bit nervous. He didn't have his nose in the air or have that know-it-all vibe to him. No, today, he could even be called shy. That alone had my interest piqued.

"Dale, come on. What's going on?" I nudged his tennis shoe with my own, trying to get him to get out of whatever funk he was in.

If anything, Dale seemed even quieter with my prodding. Pursing my lips, I grabbed my book from the ground and was about to open it, but Dale's hand caught mine, stopping me from doing so. I turned my head to ask him if he was going to tell me what the big deal was, but instead, his mouth met mine in a warm, closed-mouthed kiss.

Startled by the sudden contact, I didn't move right away. Dale must have taken it as an okay because his hand came up to cup my face, turning my head to get better access. For some reason unknown to me, I let him. It wasn't a bad kiss. In fact, it was downright toe curling but what bothered me about it was there was no pretext. I didn't even know Dale liked me that way, let alone wanted to kiss me. Most of the time I thought he thought I was just irritating. A kiss was so not something I would have guessed was coming my way.

When Dale finally broke the kiss, I was breathless, confused, and if I had to admit it, a bit turned on. Neither one of us said anything at first, but then I couldn't take it anymore.

"What the hell was that?"

Dale's brow furrowed. "I thought it was obvious. Was I that bad?"

I shook my head. "No, not bad at all. One of the best kisses I've ever had, actually."

"Then what is it? Don't you like me?" Dale shifted in his seat, his face reddening to match his hair.

"Do you like me?" I leaned forward my eyes searching his face. "I mean, don't get me wrong, I liked it, but it was just so unexpected. I didn't even know you thought of me that way."

Dale kicked the ground with his foot. "Neither did I, to be honest." He shrugged and then looked at me. The vulnerability in his eyes made my heart ache a bit.

Confused by his confession, I placed my hand on his. An unexpected tingle surged through our touching hands, but I ignored it and pushed forward. "So, what brought this on today? Someone douse you with truth serum?"

As expected, Dale's lips twisted in a disapproving frown, and he pushed his glasses up on his face. "You know there's no such thing. We can make a persuasion potion, but those at most only make someone's tongue more likely to wag freely than get the real truth from them."

I arched a brow at Dale, causing him to stop talking.

With an annoyed grunt, Dale turned his head away from me to stare out at the courtyard. Surprisingly, he never moved his hand away from mine and kept using his other hand to do things, like running his hand fingers through his already messy mop of hair.

I waited a few more moments for him to gather his thoughts. He seemed about as surprised as I was about the kiss, and based on Dale's abrasive personality, I had a feeling if I pushed it too soon, he would clam up altogether.

"So, I heard a rumor today," Dale said out of the blue. I watched him trying to figure out what that had to do with his sudden need to lay one on me.

"Oh, yeah? Was it about my fun family background?" I said sarcastically, my eyes rolling to the side. People were still talking about my last name though I had made it clear I wanted nothing to do with that side of the family.

"Did I ever apologize for that?" Dale's fingers squeezed mine, and concern etched his face.

I shook my head and smiled. "No, but I don't blame you. It was Ian after all."

Just mentioning Ian's name made Dale's face bunch up. "I'm not sure I like that guy. He's trouble."

Chuckling, I bumped his shoulder with mine. "Oh, I don't know. He seems harmless to me. A major flirt with huge brother issues but harmless none the less."

Dale snorted. "That's because you don't know him well enough. He's majoring in the Dark Arts. Those kinds of people don't do that just for the literary experience."

The warning tone in Dale's voice made me pause. Professor Piston had mentioned something about Ian belonging in the basement. Could that be where they did all the Dark Art classes? I hadn't bothered to check since I had no interest in getting in touch with the other side.

"They can't be all bad. I mean, it's not like they are raising an army to take over the world or anything." I laughed, but it was more of a nervous laugh. After all, I wasn't quite sure what I had said wasn't true.

Dale didn't laugh with me. His green eyes locked with mine with a serious intensity that it killed the little laughter I had.

"That may be true, but plenty have messed with enough blood magic to cause one to be cautious of those who decide to practice it, and Ian is in deep. Why do you think he and his brother don't get along well?"

"Because they like outdoing the other? Sibling rivalry and all that?" I offered up, trying to lighten the mood.

Shaking his head, Dale sighed. "I wished it was only that. Unfortunately, Ian got labeled as the black sheep of the family when he went into the Dark Arts rather than Potions like the rest of the Broomsteins."

"So, he decided to make his own path. That makes him bad?"

"No," Dale said and stared at the ground. "But it does make him dangerous, and I don't want to see you get hurt."

Now I was really confused. "Hold on a second, back up now. Why would you think I would get hurt?" I shifted onto my knees and turned to him. "You come waltzing down here acting all weird, and then you kiss me, and now you are warning me away from Ian. It's like I got dropped into the last half of the movie, and I don't know what's going on."

Dale gave me a sheepish look and then chuckled nervously. "My apologies, it seems I have gotten off track."

"Okay, then let's get back on track. What about this rumor?" I leaned forward on my hands, my head tilted to the side.

Dale smirked at my coy position, his hand coming up to stroke the line of my jaw. Startled by the touch, I didn't move immediately and let him do his exploring. When his fingers traced my lips, I found them parting on their own, and I was tempted to dart my tongue out to taste him.

"I can see why they want you so much," Dale murmured, his voice low like he was in some kind of trance.

"Who?" I asked, my own voice a bit husky.

"The Broomstein brothers." Dale shifted forward, his head started to dip down but before he could capture my lips again a bright flash blinded us, and a chorus of laughter followed after.

Jerking away from Dale, I rubbed my eyes and then glared up at Sabrina and her two friends. "Don't you have anything better to do?"

Sabrina shrugged a shoulder and giggled her phone in her hand. "Not really. Besides, with this," - she waved her phone with a vicious grin - "there's no way anyone will ask you to the mixer."

Ask me to the mixer? My brow scrunched together at her words. My eyes then went to Monica who stood behind Sabrina with an apprehensive look. Like she really didn't want to there. Seeing her reminded me of what Monica had told me the other day at the mall.

Ian and Paul were going to ask me to the Halloween mixer.

Suddenly, I looked at Dale. He looked a bit green in the gills, and it clicked. That was the rumor that made him kiss me and then warn me off Ian. He thought they were going to ask me out!

Glancing back to Sabrina, I waved a hand. "Go for it. See if I care. You apparently are so desperate for a date, you need to get into my business. Think of this as my gift to you." I promptly turned away from her and back to my book.

I could just imagine the blood boiling in Sabrina's veins at my dismissal. I really wanted to see it, but I restrained myself and flipped to the page I had been working on. Dale sat alert as if expecting a counter-attack at any moment.

Reaching over, I patted him on the arm. "Relax, she's not going to do anything out here in the open." I glanced over my shoulder at Sabrina meeting her gaze. "Right? You wouldn't want to ruin that perfect image of yours."

Okay, so the next thing that happened I totally asked for. Poking the snake was a bad idea, and I should have let it rest, but no, I couldn't. I had to be the one to get the last word in.

To be honest, I hadn't even realized I'd been hit with a spell until my body started to shake uncontrollably. All of a sudden, I was up on my feet and doing some weird version of the Charlton. My arms and legs jerked this way and that while everyone laughed around me.

All except Dale and Monica.

Dale jumped to his feet and grabbed my arms, trying to stop me from flailing about, but it only served to get him hit in the face.

"Sorry!" I cried out as he held his nose, annoyance, and pain covering his face.

Dale stopped trying to stop me and glared at Sabrina. "Undo it. Now."

Sabrina tapped her chin and pretended to think about it. "You know what? I don't think I remember the counterspell. I might have to run to the library and get it." She paused and grinned broadly. "Oh wait, I can't because I don't care." She flipped her hair over her shoulder and sashayed away. Libby followed after her, still giggling at the sight of me, but Monica stayed behind. Sabrina noticed right away and looked over her shoulder. "Coming, Mon?"

Monica glanced between Sabrina and me, conflicting emotions clear on her face. I could tell she wanted to help me, but she also didn't want to lose her friendship with Sabrina and thus end up in my shoes as well.

"Monica?" Sabrina turned fully back to her, her eyes narrowing.

Straightening her spine, Monica gestured to Dale. "Don't you think that's enough? Dale is one of the headmaster's assistant after. He might tell."

Sabrina seemed to think on it for a moment, her eyes going from me to Dale. Then she shrugged as if it weren't a big deal, and I fell to the ground as the spell was reversed. Dale rushed to my side, helping me to sit up.

"There, don't say I never did anything for you." Sabrina sniffed and started to stride away but paused. Putting on hand on her hip, she shifted her weight to one side. "And don't think that this means it's over."

"What's that supposed to mean?" I growled, rubbing my butt where I landed on it. "We're even. I got you, you got me."

Sabrina threw her head back and laughed. "Oh, no, honey. Not by a long shot. When I really get you, you will know. This could have all been avoided you know if you had taken my offer of friendship. Then this whole thing could have been avoided."

I gave her a confused look that caused Libby to pipe in.

"Friends don't date a friend's ex's." She nodded her head like it was something everyone knew.

"But I'm not dating him. Them. Either of them." I scrambled to my feet, my hands curled into fists. "How pathetic can you be to be throwing this big a fit over a guy you aren't even dating? That I'm not even dating. I'd understand if I were to throw Paul down and have my nasty way with him right in front of you, but this?" I scoffed in disgust, throwing my hands up in the air. "The gods themselves aren't this petty."

I expected Sabrina to go into some kind of vengeful rage, but all I got was a secretive smile. Her long legs made quick work of the courtyard between us, her skirt swishing with every movement. She didn't stop until she was inches from me.

"Don't think for a moment you know what petty is. I invented petty." Sabrina tapped her phone against my chest, and I forced back a wince.

That I couldn't argue with. Sabrina so had the vibe of being one of those who would smite you just because you walked in her path. She'd raise hell on earth over a guy. Which she was literally trying to do. I didn't know if I was afraid for Paul, or if I envied him. The scary glint in Sabrina's eyes made my decision for me.

I pitied Sabrina.

"Why did you cheat on Paul if you so clearly love him so?" I asked, startling her.

Sabrina stiffened. Hurt and regret pinched her face. As soon as it was there, it was gone, replaced by that vengeful rage I expected.

"This isn't over. You will get what's coming to you. It's not about Paul now. This is personal," Sabrina snarled at me and then stomped away, shoving through Libby and Monica who hurried after her.

Sighing, I dropped back down to the ground and started to gather my things.

Dale knelt beside me and grabbed my hand, stopping me. "What are you doing?"

"Going to class, duh." I pulled my arm away and threw my bag over my shoulder before standing up.

"But what about Sabrina? She attacked you with magic and threatened you. You can't let her get away with that." Dale had a hard tone to his voice that only made me sigh once more.

"Yes, I can." When Dale continued to follow after me even after my answer, I felt the need to explain further. "Look, I attacked her once in the library, remember? So, I can't very well tattle on her now. Besides, it wasn't anything that bad, and as for the threats. I can see where she's coming from." Dale squinted at me. "Okay, so she's kind of obsessed and crazy, but most teenage girls are. Anyway, I'm a 'deal with it as it comes' kind of gal."

"Meaning you're just gonna wait and see?" Dale scoffed, grabbing my arm to stop me. When he noticed how many students were around us, he lowered his voice. "What happens if she attacks you again? You just going to stand there and take it?"

I rolled my eyes. "Of course not. If she attacks, then I'll fight. Well, as good as I can with my underdeveloped powers." I pulled out my phone and checked the time. I had less than two minutes to class. "Look, I'll talk to you about this later. I have to get to class."

Turning on my heels, I tried to head toward my first-afternoon class but was intercepted by the headmaster.

"Ah, Miss Norman. Or are you going by Mancaster now?" Swordson stopped in front of me, his cheeks red as if he had been running.

"Still Norman," I told him, bouncing on my heel.

His eyes moved down to my feet, and he smiled. "I see you are antsy to get to class, but I'm afraid you'll be missing your afternoon classes."

I frowned. "Why's that?"

Headmaster Swordson cleared his throat and laced his fingers in front of him. "It seems you have some visitors. They are waiting in my office."

Frowning harder now, I cocked my head to the side. "Visitors? Who?" I knew it couldn't have been my parents. They were elbows deep in Egyptian sand right now.

"Seems word travels fast, not just here on campus but the magical community as well." Swordson paused for longer than normal, making me nervous. "Your grandparents are here to meet you."

My grandparents? What the hell did they want?

Chapter 16

THANKFULLY, ON THE WAY to the Headmaster's office, Dale left. Right now, my head was spinning with why my grandparents would show up out of nowhere. Dealing with Dale and his kissing would have to wait.

I followed Headmaster Swordson back to his office, feeling very much like a bad kid being sent to the principal's office. I guess it wasn't too far off though. However, what was waiting for me behind that door was not a paddle or a lecture, but some old people I'd never met before. Ones I'd never *wanted* to meet before.

"This way, Miss Norman." Headmaster Swordson opened the door for me, and I walked inside.

The two chairs that usually sat in front of the headmaster's desk were occupied. Two heads of gray hair sat with their backs to me. One who I could only assume was my grandmother had her hair twisted into a sophisticated knot on her head, an expensive-looking flower pin clipped to it. The other one had a stiff back, so stiff that I suspected someone might have shoved a stick up their spine. Or his ass. I was assuming the latter.

They didn't turn when I entered the room or when I cleared my throat. In fact, they didn't move until Headmaster Swordson sat down behind his desk and gestured over their shoulder. Then when they did move, they stood up as a unit. No twisting in chairs for them. Oh, no, that would be unsightly.

Their clothes were just as pristine as their hairstyles. My grandfather wore a suit that screamed both designer and bespoke while my grandmother wore a pale pink skirt suit along with low matching heels. They had the blue eyes that were on my mother's face and on my own. That was the only distinguishing feature that made me think they were related to me at all. If my mom looked more like them, I couldn't tell. Time had taken its toll on the pair of them.

The expression on both of their faces wasn't encouraging. They were speculating, judging, and at last disappointed.

Well, screw you too.

"This is her?" my grandmother asked, her voice stern and full of disbelief.

Before the headmaster could answer, I stepped forward, my best petulant child on my face. "Yes, this is she. What do you want?"

My grandfather snorted, lacing his fingers in front of him. "She looks exactly like her mother, and that attitude is definitely Margaret's."

"Peggy," I corrected him, earning me a disgusted look from my grandmother.

"Oh, dear god, Harold. Our child's name has been reduced to that of a dirty swine." My grandmother clasped her hand to her chest as if she were having heart palpitations.

Grandfather chuckled slightly, but it sounded more like a cough. "Come now, dear. It's been almost twenty years, you should be used to it by now. Besides, you don't want to estrange your granddaughter now that we are finally meeting her. This is our second chance." He smiled at me, a kind smile that made me think better of him and less about the stick up his butt.

My grandmother sniffed, not at all affected by my grandfather's chastising. She did, however, move closer to me, her eyes scanning me up and down. Suddenly, she grabbed my chin and turned my face this way and that.

"Hey!" I griped, jerking my face away from her. "Do you mind?"

Ignoring my question, she circled me. "At least, she's pretty. Mancaster blood, of course." She finished her full circle and stared at me. "She'll do, I suppose, but we have to do something about those clothes." My grandmother gestured two fingers at my jeans and t-shirt. "So unsightly."

"I'll have the shop set you up a line of credit," my grandfather announced, pulling his phone out of his pocket and typing in something before closing it. "There. They will be expecting you at your convenience."

"Once you have been properly dressed, we will talk about getting the official paperwork done to make you a legitimate Mancaster. Then there will be an announcement in the Daily Scribe, and we'll need to hold a party for her coming out." My grandmother ticked off the things to my grandfather, not once asking my opinion. "Of course, she's a bit old for a coming out, but it's better late than never, I suppose."

I'd had just about enough of being talked about like I wasn't there. Now, I understood why my mom left them behind.

I held my hands up and shook my head. "Woah! Hold on just one freaking second. I'm not changing my name, and I'm not buying new clothes. What I have is fine."

"But you cannot—"

"No," I snapped, cutting my grandmother off. "I am only meeting with you because it is polite, and the headmaster asked me. While I wish I could say it was nice to meet you, I have class." I started for the door.

My grandmother started to protest, but it was my grandfather who made me stop. "Maxine, please."

Those two words tugged on my heart. The desperation in those words alone froze my feet to the floor. I slowly turned back to them and, for the first time, saw the hurting in my grandfather's face. My grandmother only looked pissed off and hadn't stopped yapping.

"Nina, quiet," my grandfather barked at my grandmother, startling her. To me, his voice softened. "You'll have to forgive your grandmother, she just gets a bit ahead of herself when she's excited."

I snorted. "That was her excited?"

A hint of a smile crept up his face. "You should see her when she's upset."

Wincing, I had a feeling that wasn't something I wanted to see.

"Maybe we should start over?" my grandfather suggested, a hopeful gleam in his eyes. I glanced to Headmaster Swordson, who had been quiet this entire time, and saw a bemused expression on his face. When he saw me looking, Swordson nodded his head as if giving me the go ahead.

Sighing, I nodded. "Alright, fine. But no name changing or any other kind of changing. And I don't need a coming out party or an announcement in the Daily Scribe whatever that is."

My grandmother gasped, finally daring to speak again. "You don't even know what the Daily Scribe is? What have they been teaching you?" She shot an accusing glare at Headmaster Swordson.

"Now, now, Nina. It's not the school's responsibility to teach them all about the magical community, only how to control their powers." My grandfather placed an arm around her shoulders. "Where is your mother, by the way?"

I didn't bother asking why they didn't know. I knew they hadn't spoken since she married my dad. It would be surprising if they knew.

"Cairo. Dad has a dig."

"Still playing in the dirt, is he?" My grandmother sniffed and turned her head away. "I never understood what would possess someone to want to dig around for dead things." She shuddered.

My grandfather squeezed her close and spoke to me. "I'm assuming they left before being able to teach you the basics?"

I shrugged. "Mom taught me some, and we went to a shop to get my school supplies. She's had limited phone access since I've been at school."

My grandfather smiled. "Well, we're here now. So, feel free to ask us anything you like. Maybe we'll even give you a tour of some of the magical places right here in town."

I nodded and smiled in return. "I'd like that."

"Nina?" my grandfather asked, looking down on my grandmother.

She shifted in his arms uncomfortably and then glanced my way. "I suppose that will be alright. But only if you allow me to purchase you some new clothes."

"Nina ..."

"No," I interrupted my grandfather. "It's alright. After all, I've never had grandparents around to dote on me. Dad's live too far away. So, I figure I'm a bit overdue for some spoiling."

My grandmother rolled her eyes and let out an exasperated sigh.

"Don't mind her." My grandfather patted her on the arm. "She'll grow on you."

I wasn't sure he was right about that, but I was willing to give them the benefit of the doubt.

"Alright, we've taken up enough of your time today. I'm sure you want to go to class." My grandfather reached into his coat pocket and pulled out a business card. "Here's our address. You can come by any time. It also has my number on it, so we can set up a time for a tour and maybe dinner?"

I agreed and then took my phone out and sent him a text. "There, now you have my number."

My grandfather took out his phone and beamed down at it. "Indeed, I do. Technology. I'll never get used to it." He slipped his phone back into his pocket and then nodded to the headmaster. "Headmaster."

"Mr. Mancaster. Mrs. Mancaster. Have a pleasant evening." The headmaster stayed behind his desk, his hands folded over each other, a polite smile on his lips.

Grandfather led my grandmother to the door, but as they passed me, she grabbed my arm. "Will you think about going by Mancaster? At least, in the magical community? Please." The last word seemed painful to get out, and I had to throw her a bone.

I placed my hand on top of hers and smiled softly. "I'll think about it."

Taking my answer positively, she inclined her head and let me go. Once they were out of the door, I indicated to the headmaster I was going to leave.

"Miss Norman."

Shoving back an annoyed groan, I turned back to the older man. "Yes?"

"I heard there was a bit of disturbance during lunchtime involving you and Sabrina Craftsman. Anything I need to worry about?"

Giving him a tight smile, I shook my head. "No, nothing to worry about. Just a petty scrabble between friends. We'll figure it out on our own."

Nodding approvingly, the headmaster moved his attention to his computer. "That's what I like to hear. Have a good day."

"You too, headmaster."

I bolted out of the door before he could stop me. Once outside, I took a few deep breaths in and out. Once I had found my center once more, I kept moving. Instead of heading to class, I started toward the library. I had every intention of hiding myself away in the stacks until dinner. I'd had about enough drama for one day.

Chapter 17

THE HALLWAYS WERE PRETTY empty on my way to the library. It made the campus silent and somehow creepy. However, creepy or not, it worked for me. The fewer students I ran into, the better. It meant that they were all in class, and I wouldn't have a chance of running into Paul or Ian.

I had little doubt that the rumor going around was just a rumor, especially with what I knew about the two Broomstein brothers. More than likely one of them found out that the other was going to ask me, and so the other decided to do it as well.

Well, they had another thing coming. I wasn't going to give them the chance to ask. I would just avoid them both until the Halloween Mixer, and that would solve that. This would mean that I would have to bring out my stealth ninja skills. I had to be alert at all times, keeping an eye out for enemy forces. Maybe I should find out their schedules? Then it would be easy to make sure I wasn't where they were.

Except I already knew one place I couldn't avoid Paul. Professor Piston's class. I groaned and scuffed my feet on the ground. Since Paul was Piston's teacher's assistant, it would be near impossible to keep away from him. Maybe I could just make sure I got there right as the class starts so that he won't have a chance to talk to me. Then, as soon as class was over, I would run like a bat out of hell.

I continued grumbling to myself on the way to the library, trying to figure out the best way to stay out of the sight of the Broomstein brother for another few days. Unfortunately for me, that meant I wasn't really using my ninja skills to be aware of my surroundings, which also meant I didn't see the very focus of my thoughts standing right outside the library doors until it was too late.

"Max, what a delightful surprise." Ian smirked at me, moving off the wall he had been leaning on.

My eyes widened, and I stopped in my tracks. For a moment, I almost broke my vow to pretend they didn't exist and then I remembered. Ducking my head down, I quickened my pace. I almost made it into the library, but Ian was quicker than me, jumping into my path and blocking my entrance.

"Now, don't be that way." Ian frowned, his arms crossed over his chest as he tried to fill the whole doorway. "I just want to talk."

"I'm busy. Go away." I sidestepped to duck around him, but he moved with me. We danced for a moment, me going one way and then another only to be blocked by Ian every time. Sighing in defeat, I placed my hands on my hips and tapped my foot. "What will it take to get you to move?"

Ian grasped his head with a grin. "Do I sense a bit of déjà vu? Didn't we do this before?"

I grimaced. I had said those very words to him before, and as I recalled, the price was exactly what I wanted to prevent. I contemplated pretending to give him what he wanted but then thought better of it.

"Forget it. I'll just go study in my room." I turned to leave, but a hand clamped down on my shoulder.

This time, Ian's voice lost its playful conceited tone when he called my name. It made me want to hear what he had to say. Rubbing a hand over my face, I cursed my big heart.

"Look," I started, forcing my voice to soften. "It's not that I don't like you. I mean,

I hardly know you, and while you are nice to look at, you come with a lot of drama. Namely, your brother. So, if you don't mind, I'd rather we didn't."

Ian had begun to smile halfway through my explanation, and I had a feeling my words had gone in one ear and out the other.

"So, you think I'm nice to look at?" He puffed up his chest and gave me a salacious look. "Just nice? I don't think I've ever been called that before. Hot, sexy, panty melting, but nice?" He sighed dramatically and lifted his hands up. "It seems I need to up my game if that's all I'm putting out there."

"Of course, that's the only part you paid any attention to." I rolled my eyes and moved to leave again. Once more, my path was blocked by Ian's muscular form. "Ugh, how are you doing that? You can't possibly be that fast."

"Magic, honey. Magic." He winked at me. When I didn't grin in response, his smile dropped. "Fine. You want the truth?"

"That would be refreshing." I crossed my arms under my breasts and shifted my weight to one side as I waited for this so-called truth from him.

Ian inched closer to me, his hands in his pockets and his face pointed downward. "I've never met a girl like you. I mean, besides the obvious attraction I feel, you're not like the other females on campus."

"You mean, I'm not ensorcelled by your charm and good looks?"

His hand clutched his heart in mock dismay. "You wound me, but yes, that is part of it. Another reason is because you didn't grow up in this world. You don't know your protective magic from your defensive magic."

"So, it's because I'm a unique being? Something you can say you did and put in your record book?" I bit out, not liking the way he was talking about me.

Ian quickly became defensive. "No, no. That's not what I mean at all. I mean ..." He sighed dejectedly, dragging a hand through his dark hair. "I'm not explaining this right, am I?"

I watched him curiously, trying to figure out what exactly he was trying to say.

"What I mean to say ... is you don't judge. You don't look at me and see ..." He waved a hand over himself with desolate eyes. "... what everyone else sees. You just see me."

I pursed my lips and stared at him. "What am I supposed to see? You just look like you."

"See!" Ian pointed at me, getting excited. "That. Exactly that. You don't see that I'm different, and that's what I like." Ian shook

231

his head and chuckled bitterly. "Most girls won't date me."

That surprised me. I thought he had all kinds of admirers. He definitely looked like one of those guys who could get any girl he wanted.

"Surprising, I know, right?" Ian gave a wry grin. "But if any of the girls here were interested in me, it's for a one night only experience. I'm just something they can say they did."

When he quoted my words back at me, I winced. Okay, now I felt bad.

"So, why don't they want to date you?" I relaxed slightly, no longer ready to bolt. I wasn't even going to think about the fact that I'd pretty much forgot about my mission.

"Let's just say that I don't meet their criteria for a perfect wizard," Ian said evasively. "Anyway, I wanted to see if you had a date for the mixer this weekend?"

And there it was. The reason I was avoiding him, to begin with. Now, though, I felt bad for the guy and didn't want to flat out tell him no. After all, he liked me because I wasn't like the others. Though I wasn't exactly sure why they didn't want to be with him, anyway. Those girls were crazy.

Griping my bag strap, I shifted it back up on my shoulder. "No, I don't have a date." I could see the hope in his eyes, and I hated to kill it. "But I planned on going with Trina. You know, as a girl's night."

"A girl's night? For a mixer?" Ian cocked his head to the side, clearly confused.

I grinned at him. "Isn't the whole point of the mixer to get to know other people? If I come with a date, then how am I going to do that? I would feel like a dick if I didn't hang around them the entire time, but then I would be missing out on the best part of the event."

Ian nodded. "I understand. So, no date. How about instead, I'll see you there?"

"Sure." I beamed up at him.

He reached out and brushed my hair from my face, making my skin tingle. "Save me a dance? A slow one."

Giggling like a silly school girl, I bit my lower lip and nodded. "Sure. I can do that." I watched as Ian walked away from me, and I would be lying if I didn't check out his butt as he went. That boy sure was hot. Definitely what Callie would call one of the local hotties.

My face heating with my thoughts, I spun around and headed into the library. I hadn't completely kept to my plan, but I also hadn't given in. I hadn't promised Sabrina anything, but I also didn't want to cause more problems than I already had. Promising Ian a dance wasn't the same thing as showing up with him at the mixer. This way, I wasn't picking any of them, and I could still have fun.

As I made my way into the main part of the library, my eye caught the other Broomstein brother. So, neither of them had been in class? I guess it paid to be an upperclassman.

Instead of hiding in the stacks, I walked straight toward Paul and sat down across from him. I didn't look at him as I unpacked my things and opened my book to study. I could feel his eyes on me, and I wondered how long it would take before he asked me to go to the mixer.

Surprisingly, Paul didn't speak up for a good ten minutes, and when he did, it had nothing to do with the mixer. "So, I heard Sabrina was being a bitch to you again this morning. I'm sorry."

I kept my eyes on my book and shrugged. "Nothing to be sorry for. She's in charge of her own actions. Why should you feel responsible?"

Paul sighed, his pen clacking on the table. "Because I know she's only bullying you because of me."

"You mean because she's still in love with you?" I landed my sharp gaze on him, daring him to deny it.

Leaning back in his seat, Paul shook his head. "She's not, you know. In love with me, I mean."

I scoffed. "Could have fooled me."

"She's good at that. Fooling people into believing what she wants." Paul tapped his fingers on the arms of the chair. "She's obsessed with appearances and believes she and I would make the best couple on the outside. However, believe me, that's the only interest she has in me. Political."

"Because you're a Broomstein and she's a Craftsman?" I asked, trying to piece it all together. Though I was literally in the same town as my old life, it felt like I was in a completely different country. I had to learn everything from scratch.

"Yeah, something like that." Paul rocked his chair back and forth on its hind legs. "But really, neither of us were happy while we were dating. Any of the times. If we ended up getting married ..." He paused and shuddered, letting his chair fall back to the floor with a loud thud. "I couldn't imagine the level of hell that would be, let alone for any of our children."

"Then why do it?" I leaned forward on my elbows. "Why pretend she wants you if she knows just as well as you that it wouldn't work?"

Paul gave me a weary smile. "Her parents. If Sabrina is anything, she's a dutiful daughter."

I frowned at that. "Really? She would go to the lengths of perusing a guy simply because her parents wanted her too? Even if she doesn't even like him?"

"Yep."

"What kind of masochistic crap is that?" I gaped at him and sat back in my chair. I loved my parents more than anything in the world, but to go so far? No way. Of course, my parents would never think of asking such a thing of me. My grandparents, however … the way my grandmother had started to plan my life right before my eyes told me they would definitely do something like this. At least, she would.

I'd have to be careful of her. No matter how much she was trying to let me be myself, there was a reason my mom didn't want anything to do with them.

Paul made a sort of snort laugh, and my eyes jerked up to him. "What?"

"Nothing," he chuckled, shaking his head. "Just watching your face as you think. I sometimes forget that you didn't grow up with this stuff."

"And that's a terrible thing?"

"No, it's a good thing actually," Paul murmured, his eyes becoming focused on the table. "You have no idea how much of a relief it is to have someone talk to you without having to think about what they are trying to get out of you and your family. I know with you, you're only just talking." He offered me a smile that made my heart flutter.

"You know," I started not sure if I really should bring it up or not but decided to anyway, "your brother said something similar to me. You two aren't as different as you think."

I expected Paul to get angry or to start talking crap about his brother, but instead, there was nothing but sadness on his face. "I get that. For an outsider, our problems might seem frivolous, but just like Sabrina, we are all bound by our family name and the privileges come with obligations. Even if we don't like them."

"So, you're an ass to each other because your parents say so?" My brows furrowed as I stared at him in disbelief. When he nodded sullenly, I wanted to smack him. "I'm sorry, but that's stupid. He's your bother. So, what if he made some choices you don't agree with? He's still your brother." I shook my head in disgust. "I would have loved to have a brother, any kind of sibling really. To have someone to turn to and know no matter what they will always be there for you? The fact that you have that but shove it aside? It's unforgivable."

"Really?" Paul arched a brow. "You find that so offensive? Even if that sibling did something that was dangerous and marred your family's name?"

I snorted. "If it's dangerous, I'd make sure I was there to pull his ass out of the fire. Who better to watch my back than a sibling? Besides, who cares about what people think? You're all going to die someday, and do you really think anyone is going to remember anything we do now?"

Paul quieted. He had a tense and focused expression on his face. His thoughts ran across his eyes a mile a minute. Finally, after a long moment, he spoke again.

"You know, I wished I'd met you before." He smiled softly at me. "I could have used someone like you when this whole thing started."

"Well, I'm here now. Kicking butts and saving families." I gave him a thumbs-up and stuck my tongue out, causing him to laugh. I really loved that sound.

Standing to his feet, Paul put his books away and then looked at me. "You know, I had every intention of asking you to the mixer today before my brother got a chance, but I think now I would rather him have you and be happy than for me to stand in his way."

My heart thudded loudly in my chest and my throat constricted. Wetting my lips, I stared up at him. "Actually, your brother already asked me."

"Oh?" I was pretty sure he was going for curious and not dejected, but he didn't quite make it there. I could tell that even though he wanted to let his brother have a chance with me, he wanted me for himself as well. I wasn't sure how I felt about that. Flattered for one. I'd never had so many guys interested in me at the same time. I was lucky to have one even look my way. Now that I was so popular, it was a bit overwhelming.

Tucking my hair behind my ear, I answered, "Yeah, just before I came here."

"Well, I'm happy for him. I mean, you. Both of you." Paul stumbled over his words, making me giggle. "Please just kill me now."

"Well, I don't know about that, but while I did say he asked me, I didn't say I said yes." I watched Paul's face go from confusion to excitement and then he quickly covered it up with a useless frown.

"Why? I mean, why did you say no?" Paul shifted in place as if he couldn't stay still. He shoved his hand into his pocket, trying to still himself to no avail.

I lifted a shoulder and dropped it. "It's a mixer. It doesn't make sense to bring a date."

"Oh," Paul said and then added, "So, I guess I'll see you there?"

Unable to stop the grin from curving up my lips, I nodded. "I guess you will."

Chapter 18

"I'M NOT GOING." TRINA paced the room, chewing on her nails until they were down to the quick.

"It'll be fine. Stop stressing." I leaned toward the mirror so I could apply my mascara.

"Pfft. Says you." Trina stopped pacing long enough to glare at me. "You've got three guys dying to take you out on that dance floor while I have nothing but an ulcer developing." She rubbed her stomach and used the bed to hold herself up. She had been freaking out for the last few days because she hadn't had the guts to ask Libby to the mixer. Now, she would have to go to the mixer alone – well, with me - and hope that she could ask Libby to dance.

"I told you, we could just go together."

"No way, I'm not going to be your buffer." Trina scoffed and rolled her eyes. "You just don't want to have to face all those hungry guys just waiting to eat you up." She chuckled and pulled on her heels. She'd done some kind of spell that made her hair slick and straight. A yellow flower decorated her hair and matched the skin-tight dress that flowed around her legs when she moved. She looked great.

"You have no reason to be nervous. Libby is going to think you are hot." I adjusted the top of my pale blue dress. I found a pair of sparkly white shoes to add to the ensemble, and I was ready.

"Look at you." Trina grinned, looking me up and down. "Those guys won't know what to do with themselves. So, tell me, which one do you like?"

I busied myself with searching for my bag under my bed. "I don't know what you mean."

Trina plopped down on my bed and smacked me on the hip. "You know exactly what I mean." When I didn't answer, she bounced harder. "Come on, you have to have one that you like more than the other. I bet it's Ian. He's got that bad boy thing going on, and I hear he's great in bed."

"Pfft." I chuckled and shook my head. "There's more to someone than just how good in bed they are." I paused and then grinned.

"Like how good their butt looks as they are walking away from you."

Cackling, Trina rocked back and forth on the bed holding her stomach like it was the funniest thing she had ever heard.

"But to be honest, I like them all." I sighed, shoving my lip gloss and phone into my bag. "Well, what I know of them. I haven't gone out with any of them yet. Not really."

"Well, you better figure it out fast because one reason I like girls is that guys tend to have the whole pee-on-everything-I-think-that-belongs-to-me philosophy. Too messy." Her nose scrunched up, and she waved her hands in front of her. "It would be funny to see them throw down for you though."

I snorted and headed for the door. "I don't think that's going to happen. If anyone is going to throw down, it will be Sabrina and me. She's so hung up on Paul and her having a happily ever after that if he even looks my direction, she'll throw a huge fit."

"So, you're gonna steer clear of him?" Trina asked, watching my face curiously.

I gave her a sideways glance. "What do you think?"

Trina giggled and looped her arm with mine. "That's my girl."

You could hear the music from the quad before you even got there. The headmaster had the service staff set up a buffet table and decorate the area with Halloween decorations. Except these weren't anything like the ones I'd seen back in high school.

The skeletons weren't just hanging on the wall, they were dancing around on the makeshift dance floor. The jack-o'-lanterns glowed from within with magical flames that couldn't be put out, and the ceiling was a starry sky with a full moon. It was the perfect setting to meet someone.

"Wow." I gaped and slowly moved into the room, trying to take it all in. "So, this is what a real magical party looks like."

Trina giggled. "Come on, you'll get used to it." She dragged me further into the room and started grinning and waving at people we knew. I kind of just followed her, still in a daze from the room, the environment, just everything.

I stared down at the punch bowl that poured glasses of punch on their own before handing them to waiting students. I didn't know what Trina was talking about, there's no way I'd get used to this anytime soon.

"Look!" Trina whispered in my ear. "There's Libby."

I followed where she was pointing to where Libby stood with Sabrina and Monica. They were all dressed to kill in what had to be designer dresses and heels that had to have cost ten times what I paid for my own.

"Doesn't she look gorgeous?" Trina practically bounced next to me with excitement.

"Yeah and so do you, so go talk to her." I untangled her arm from mine and pushed her in Libby's direction. I watched as she started toward the blonde, sipping from my glass. Unfortunately, Trina only made it five feet before she bypassed Libby completely and darted into the bathroom. Shaking my head, I sighed. She'd get it, eventually.

"Hey Max, you look really great."

I turned to see Dale standing beside me. His hair was slicked back, and his glasses were missing. Add that to his button-down shirt and dress slacks and any girl would be drooling, me included.

"You too," I got out after swallowing my mouth full of punch. "I didn't think you were into these kinds of things?" I gestured around with my head.

Dale tucked his hands in his pockets and ducked his head sheepishly. "Well, I'm not, but I knew you'd be here."

Ah, there it was. My face heated, and I thanked the dim lighting that hid it.

"So, how are you enjoying your first wizard party?" Dale took a glass from the table, not at all awed by the magic keeping it going.

"Why do you call it that?" I couldn't help but ask. "Why not a witch party? There are both males and females at this party." I took a drink of my cup and then used it to circle the room. "Why can't there be a gender-neutral name?"

Dale seemed at a loss for words, and for a moment, he started to stumble for something to say that wouldn't offend me. I couldn't take it anymore and burst out laughing and smacking him on the arm. "I'm sorry, I'm just messing with you."

Frowning, Dale stared at me for a second and then smiled slightly. "You're funny."

I shrugged a shoulder. "I try. Doesn't always land where I want it to though."

"I have to say I'm surprised to see you here alone." Dale scanned the room, clearly searching for some mystery date. "Did the Broomsteins not ask you?"

"Oh, they did." Dale's face dropped, My heart ached for a second, and I couldn't mess with him anymore. "But I told them I wanted to take the chance to meet the other students, and I couldn't do that if I had a guy hanging around me the entire time."

Dale's eyes lifted and widened slightly. "Oh, am I doing that? Am I the guy?"

"No, no. I didn't mean you. Not that I'm saying I'm here with you, but I don't mind standing here talking to you." I offered him a smile which he gave back to me a bit shyly. It was funny how different Dale was from the first day I met him. He had been so abrasive and ready to hit me where it hurt with his prejudice against the privileged students. Now, he was so insecure about himself around me but at the same time still abrasive, if that kiss and his clear need to keep me away from Ian were anything to go by.

"Would it have bothered you if I had come with someone?" I was curious to see how he would react. Would he be jealous? Was he trying to piss on me like Trina said, marking me as his territory?

However, he completely surprised me. Dale simply shrugged, more relaxed than I'd seen him in a while. "No. I mean, I don't have a claim to you. We aren't dating. I don't even know if you like me, even though I clearly stated my intentions. You did get that from the kiss, right?" His eyes bored into mine, searching for some sign that I understood him.

I moved closer to Dale and placed my hand on his arm. "Yes, I got that, and I like you too, but like you said, we've never gone out." I paused and smiled coyly. "Maybe we should remedy that, don't you think?"

Dale nodded rapidly. "Yes, yes. I think we should."

"Great." I tapped him on the nose. "I'll text you." Leaving it at that, I moved toward the bathroom where Trina had reappeared.

"Looks like you had no problem getting a date," Trina grumbled, taking my cup from my hand and downing it. "I wish I had your confidence."

I laughed. "Oh, believe me. I'm just making this up as I go along. Besides, Dale's nice." I flashed her a grin. "By the way, you're wrong about the pissing contest."

"Oh, really?" she leaned away from me, her brows raised.

"Yep. Dale didn't seem to have a problem with me seeing other guys. Not that I'd decided to go out with anyone else just to be clear. Just nice to have options." It was pretty relieving, to be honest. The only meaningful relationship I'd had was with Jaron, and he had been all too quick to let everyone know that I belonged to him. At the time, I found it endearing. I felt wanted. Now a part of me was glad he dumped me. There was something better waiting for me. Several someones, as a matter of fact, and one of them was walking toward me right now.

"Ian," I cooed, my eyes openly ogling him. The black button-up shirt went well with the leather pants he was sporting. If anyone ever looked like he belonged out and about on Halloween, it was him.

Ian wrapped his arms around my waist and drew me to him. The over-familiar action made my blood pulsing through my veins. "Maxine, you look absolutely ravishing." He glanced over my shoulder at Trina and winked. "You too, Trina. You talk to Libby yet?"

"Oh my god, does everybody know?" Trina cried out and stomped her feet, no doubt feeling completely mortified.

"No, they don't," Ian assured her. "I've just been staring at Max for the last twenty minutes and noticed you were staring at Libby the same way. Kind of easy to put two and two together."

Trina settled down and answered, "Oh. Well, that's good. I think."

"Look, Sabrina and Monica are dancing." Ian pointed toward the trio. "Here's your chance." Trina didn't have to be told twice before she was on the move.

I smiled up at him surprised. "That was nice of you."

"Oh, don't think too highly of me." Ian grinned back. "I did it for purely selfish reasons." When I looked at him confused, he pressed his forehead to mine and drew my hands into his. "You still owe me a dance, and look at that, it's a slow one."

Giggling, I let him guide me along until we were on the dance floor. We swayed back and forth to the music, Ian's hard body pressed against mine, causing all sorts of tingles to run through my body. I started talking, as much to distract myself from what I was feeling as any need to speak.

I started pulling Ian's attention back to me. "So, you were watching me, huh?"

"Yes, I was." Ian smirked, and his eyes flicked to where Dale watched us now. "So, you like that type of guy?"

I lifted a shoulder. "Sometimes, but right now, I like your type."

Ian chuckled and spun me around before pulling me back to him. "And what type is that?"

"I'm not sure yet," I murmured, our faces close enough to feel each other's breath. "You're conceited and yet sensitive. Funny and charming. However, you can be kind of a jerk."

"Oh, now that one hurt." Ian nodded, his lips pursing. "You know, I'm not that bad a guy when you get to know me."

"Oh, I heard." I grinned up at him. "Several girls have known you and have plenty to say."

"All good, I hope?" The shit-eating grin on his face was so adorable that I could have kissed him. I would have too, had his brother not shown up at that precise moment.

"Mind if I cut in?" Paul asked, his eyes on his brother. The way he had been talking about backing off for Ian made me think Paul wouldn't approach me at all. Seemed like he couldn't make himself stay away.

Ian simply smiled at him. "For you, brother? Of course." Ian took my hand and brought it up to his mouth, giving it a long, wet kiss. "I will see you later on?"

I nodded and smiled. As Ian stalked away, I let my eyes wander to the back of his pants. Man, that boy was fine.

"I see my brother has thoroughly charmed you." Paul offered me his hand, the expression on his face unreadable. I couldn't tell if he was upset by this or not. I guess there was only one way to find out.

"Don't laugh at me for the asking, but how does that make you feel?" I cocked my head to the side and placed my hand on his shoulder, letting him hold the other one.

"Disappointed. Annoyed. Regretful. And a bit relieved." Paul's lips tipped up at the ends. "I'm glad someone finally sees him the way I've seen him all these years, even if it is the girl that I like as well. If anyone should win, it should be him."

I frowned at this. "And why can't you both win? Why does it have to be all or nothing?"

Paul's face scrunched up in confusion. "I don't know, to be honest. I guess that's the way I always saw it, and everyone made me believe it had to be that way. There are no ties. Only winners and losers."

"Pfft. Now that sounds like something your parents would say." I let myself sink into his embrace and just enjoyed his company. It wasn't the same as Ian, but I didn't like to compare them. They both caused a spark in me in their own ways, and there was no way I could find the imbalance between the two of them.

"That *is* something my parents would say and have said." Paul didn't seem very happy about that. "However, Ian has been on the losing side far more than they would like, and I would like to see him have a win for once." Paul's hand came up to cup my face. The raw sincerity there touched me so deeply, I forgot all about being in the middle of a crowded room with Sabrina not five feet away.

Then I did something I never expected to do. I kissed him.

Chapter 19

I DIDN'T MEAN FOR it to happen. I certainly didn't plan it. However, I couldn't get those puppy dog eyes out of my head, and my lips acted accordingly.

Thankfully, Paul reacted right away, his hands cupping my face and pulling me closer. My fingers tangled in his hair and a small part of my brain noted it was as soft as it looked. It wasn't even a passionate kiss. There was no tongue wiggling or exchanged of saliva. Only our mouths pressed against one another, and it seemed like it went on forever.

Unfortunately, that meant that everyone and their mom had time to see us locking lips on the dance floor, including one crazy-as-hell ex-girlfriend. She was the one who ripped us apart, her nails digging into my arm as she jerked me away.

"What did I tell you? What did I tell you?" Sabrina screeched for all to hear. "I told you to stay away from him or else, and you blatantly kiss him right in front of me? Do you have a death wish, Norman?"

I calmly wiped my mouth, making a show of fixing my lip gloss before sighing. "Sabrina, you really need to get over yourself. Sometimes a kiss is just a kiss. It has nothing to do with you."

Paul came over and put his arm around me with a death glare pointed at Sabrina. "Exactly what Max said. This is none of your business."

Sabrina gaped at us. "None of my business? Did you hear that all? The great Broomstein thinks our future is none of my business! Well, let me tell you something, buddy." She shoved a finger into Paul's chest with every word. "It *is* my business because our families have an agreement. Just because you don't value family the same way I do doesn't mean that I will let you renege on that promise. And you!" Sabrina looked me up and down like I was last week's trash. "First Dale, and now Paul? And was that Ian I saw you with a bit ago as well? You just don't have a solid, decent bone in your pathetic body, do you?"

Okay, things were going too far. Who did this girl think she was? What I did and who

I did it with was none of her business, and it was high time she learned her place.

"Yeah, that's right." I sneered at her. "I can kiss whoever I want, and there's nothing you can do about it." Then I did something that was a long time coming.

Sabrina stumbled backward on her high heels, and her friends caught her before she fell. When she came back, she was beyond livid and crackling with magic. The hairs on my arm stood on end, and for a moment, I regretted my actions.

"You think you're some hot shot now that you're a witch?" Sabrina boomed. In response to her voice, the night sky above us turned dark, and lightning cracked. When the lightning left the sky and hit the music station, causing sparks to fly, the students screamed and started to scatter. A few stupid ones hung around, waiting to see what would happen next, but the majority of them ran out of the quad. Hopefully, to tell a teacher or even the headmaster that there was a broken witch wreaking havoc on the locals.

"You're not just going to stand there and take that, are you?" Trina appeared at my side, her hand on my arm. "She's going to fry you like a corn dog if you don't fight back."

"What do you expect me to do?" I glanced back at her nervously. "I've barely mastered transfiguration. Weather manipulation is so out of my league."

"But if you don't do something, she'll know she beat you. You'll always have to watch your back and say goodbye to your budding romances." She gestured toward Paul who was trying to get through the whirlwind Sabrina had created to talk her down.

Fuck. Who knew the witch bitch would turn into the evil sea witch with just a taste of her own medicine. I had to stop her. But how?

Every time I'd done large scale magic, I had been upset, angry even, but now I wasn't angry. Sure, I was a bit irritated that Sabrina interrupted us but not mad. In fact, I felt pity for her and concern for the bystanders.

How could I gather power to match hers? The only time I'd felt my internal energy grow so strong was during one of my accidents and ... during my daily stretches! Every time I did power poses, the ball of magic inside of me grew so large it hurt my head. That had to be what I needed to do to beat her.

Kicking my heels off, I put my feet together and took a deep breath before releasing it as I brought my hands down. I continued to do it again as Trina gaped at my side.

"You're stretching? Now? Don't you think that's a bit inappropriate?" Trina waved a hand at Sabrina who had started to throw stuff in our direction with her magic. Paul had gotten knocked to the side, and I couldn't see Dale or Ian anywhere. They probably did the smart thing and high tailed it out of here.

"Just give me a moment, you'll see," I reassured Trina as I shifted one foot back and the other forward, bringing my hands to my chest as I closed my eyes. Breathing deeply, I focused on that ball of light in my head. I urged it to grow bigger, to help me fight against Sabrina and all she represented.

At first, the light didn't do much of anything, but maybe that was because of my desperation calling to it, or maybe it was just as annoyed by Sabrina's hissy fit. Eventually, the light grew. It grew rapidly and uncontrollably. For the first time, it didn't just stay in my head, it spread throughout my body, and my veins were on fire. My head ached from the speed in which my power consumed me. I knew I wouldn't be able to hold it for long, not at this rate. I was too new to the craft. Too inexperienced. It would burn me up long before I could focus it properly.

"Holy shit on a cracker, Max!" Trina cried out beside me, taking a step back. "You're glowing. Like your eyes are literally balls of light." The awe in her voice was laced with fear, and part of my magic liked that. It wanted to be adored but at the same time let those who would oppose us know what was coming.

I raised my hand up slowly, and with barely a thought, the wind died down. The sky above us changed back to the charmed night sky, and Sabrina stood alone in the middle of the wreckage. She gaped at me for a moment, unable to believe I had stopped her little bitch fit. Then she clamped her mouth closed and narrowed her eyes at me.

"So, you want to play in the big leagues, do you? Little whittle Maxine Norman is ready to put her human ways behind and fight like a witch, huh?" Sabrina cackled and strode toward me. "Well, let me give you your first taste!" A powerful force hit me unexpectedly, throwing me to the ground, Sabrina's laughter filling my ears all the way down.

I got back up on my feet just as quickly as I went down. But just as soon as I stood back up, she was throwing things at me. I could only use my magic to create a barrier in front of me. I couldn't even get a hit in.

"Have you had enough, yet? Or maybe we should turn up the heat?" Sabrina held her hand up as a ball of fire appeared in her hand. The red and orange glow from it caused her already crazed face to look like that of a literal devil. I had a moment to think about how much this was going to sting before I remembered that I was a freaking witch. If she could make a fire, I could put out those flames.

I tried to replicate what Sabrina did and call up the winds to blow the flame out, but it only ended up knocking me off my feet. Sabrina's laughter filled my ears, making my anger spark hotter.

"Look at you. How pathetic. I don't even need to kill you, you'll do it yourself." Sabrina cackled and pointed at me, too absorbed in laughing at me to notice I had changed the clouds above us.

This time instead of a lightning storm, the clouds grew heavy and dark, and a moment later they broke open with a deluge of rain on top of Sabrina. She screeched as the rain doused her fireball as well as her hair and dress. She seemed more upset about her dress than the fire, to be honest.

"What the hell is your problem?" she yelled at me. "This cost a fortune, and you've ruined it!"

Rolling my eyes, I flicked my finger toward her, imagining her legs were bowling pins I wanted to knock over. To my satisfaction, her legs crumbled beneath her and stopped any kind of repercussions she planned. Thankfully, I didn't have to listen to her wailing for very long because Dale hurried back into the room with Professor Piston and the Headmaster following him. They took one look at the scene and were obviously unsure of who to blame.

"It's her fault." Sabrina pointed a finger at me, her eyes welling up with fake tears. "She attacked me!"

Professor Piston took one look at Sabrina and dismissed us. Instead, he turned to the students hiding behind the tables. "It's alright now. You can come out. The party is over. Everyone, return to your dorm rooms."

The students lingered at first, wanting to get a good look, and that no doubt caused Piston to shout. "Out, now!" The students hustled out the door, stumbling over themselves to get away from the grumpy professor.

Headmaster Swordson stood by Sabrina, listening to her gripe about me. Libby and Monica hurried to her side when they could and helped her to her feet. I worried that the headmaster might believe her over me, but my view of them was blocked by a large looming form.

"Here."

I glanced up to see Aidan standing over me, offering me a hand. Sighing with exhaustion, I placed my hand in his and allowed him to bring me to my feet. The room spun out of control, and I ended up leaning against Aidan's hard chest to keep my balance.

"Too much magic isn't good for the body." Aidan's stiff explanation made me laugh.

"Tell me about it." I giggled and tried to clear my head. Things had stopped spinning, but I felt weak. Like I hadn't eaten in days, and my body was shutting down on me.

"You should rest. Here." He shoved a plastic wrapped bar into my hand. "Eat."

I looked down at the protein bar in my hand, and my stomach gurgled in protest. "I don't know if I can."

"It's okay, I'll help her." Ian appeared next to Aidan and took the bar from my hand. Dale showed up next, bringing a chair with him for me to sit down.

"You guys are too good to me." I murmured as Ian offered me small bites of the protein bar. "You shouldn't be."

"And why not?" Paul asked, kneeling at my side. "You did what most people longed to do but were too afraid. You stood up to Sabrina."

"And got knocked on my ass for it." I laughed weakly. My eyes slowly moved to where the headmaster talked to Sabrina clearly trying to calm her down. "And if she has her way, expelled."

"Not going to happen." Dale shook his head and patted me on the shoulder. "Sabrina can spin whatever tale she wants, but there was a room full of people who saw her throw the first spell. If anyone gets expelled, it'd be her."

Ian snorted. "Fat chance. The Craftsmans have their fingers too deep in the headmaster's pockets. He's not going to expel their only daughter. He might give her a slap on the wrist, but that's about it."

I sighed. The influence of the rich. I guess I couldn't complain. I'd all but rejected my own rich family. If I had taken their help and their name, things might have been different. Until then, I would just plead my case and hope I didn't get in too much trouble.

As if knowing we were talking about him, Headmaster Swordson walked up to Aidan's side. "Well, look at this. You have Broomstein, Varens, and Templars rushing to your side." The headmaster grinned down at me. "That is quite the set of knights here, Miss Norman."

"She didn't start it," Dale quickly said though no one asked.

Headmaster Swordson chuckled. "I am well aware of the situation but thank you, Mr. Varens." We all looked at the headmaster curiously. His eyes crinkled around the edges, and he tapped his head. "I didn't become the headmaster of such a school on looks alone. It does take a bit of brain to run such a large establishment. Rest assured, Miss Norman, I will be dealing with Miss Craftsman accordingly. I just ask that you work on keeping your nose out of trouble." He glanced around the group of guys, a bemused expression on his face. "Though I'm sure that might be easier said than done."

"I will try my best, headmaster." I smiled weakly up at him.

He nodded and left, no doubt to check on the damage Sabrina and I had caused.

"So, think you can walk now?" Paul asked, offering me a hand. I let him help me up, and this time, I was happy to see that I could stand without the room going nuts.

"I think I'm good. I just need to sleep." I slowly walked out of the circle of guys, and my eyes landed on Sabrina. She was still screeching to anyone who would listen, which seemed to only be Libby and Monica right now. Monica looked my way and gave me a sort of nod. A nod that I took as a sign of respect and friendship.

As Sabrina left with Libby and Monica to lick her wounds, I realized I might not be the worst witch there. In fact, I kicked ass. There wasn't anything I couldn't do now. Well, that might be going a bit far. I was still human after all. Or well, a witch. It was all still so very confusing. Changing species at the peak of your life was hard enough, but the fact that I was no longer at the bottom of the food chain made the whole thing worth it.

I couldn't wait to tell Callie!

Chapter 20

SO, I JUST HAVE to say that being the big witch on campus was awesome. After the showdown with Sabrina, everyone knew my name. Well, they knew the Mancaster name. I still had to remind people I go by Norman. In any case, it was freaking great.

People were holding the door for me. Asking me to help them with their homework, not that I could really help most of them. I was still new myself. Still, being asked was pretty flattering.

Also, I never lacked for someone to eat with at lunch. Everyone wanted to be my friend, and it was awesome. Well, it was for about a week, and then I started having to hide. I studied in my room. Sent Trina for books when I needed them from the library. I even lost a couple of pounds from skipping meals just so I could get some alone time!

It was getting freaking ridiculous. Really, I didn't know how Sabrina did it. Well, I knew how she did it. She ruled with an iron fist. Or rather by being a bitch. People adored her, and yet they feared her.

I was never that good at making people afraid. I'd never had a calling for it. I just wanted everyone to like everyone else and live in harmony. However, I also wasn't a naïve nitwit and knew that was hardly realistic.

"Can you believe it's winter break already?" Trina asked, shoving the last of her things into her bag.

"Yeah, it's pretty crazy." I laid back on my bed, delaying the inevitable. I hated packing. I mean, I only lived a few minutes away so there wasn't any reason to pack, but I also didn't trust leaving my stuff here for the next two weeks. Not that I didn't think the school was safe. No, it was the students I didn't trust. Not everyone goes home for break, and those that didn't might think it's funny to mess with my things.

Namely, Sabrina.

I wasn't a hundred percent sure she was staying, but on the off chance that she was, I had little doubt she didn't have thoughts of payback in her mind. After all, I did kick her off her pedestal. I'd be looking for some revenge of my own if I were in her shoes.

"Aren't you going to pack? Your parents will be here any minute." Trina smacked my leg with her shirt before throwing it into the bag.

"I know." I sighed and sat up. "It's just hard to leave."

Trina snorted. "And here I thought you couldn't wait to get away? Or are you going to miss all your adoring fans?"

I chuckled and shook my head. "No, I'm not going to miss that. Being popular is great, but it gets annoying. I kind of want to go back to the way it was. Even with Sabrina's bullying."

Gasping in mock horror, Trina sat down on her bed, her hand on her chest. "Even with the bullying? Really?"

"Shut up." I stuck my tongue out at her. "It wasn't that bad. At least, I knew who my real friends were and had some time to actually do my work. I want to learn magic and keep myself from blowing someone up, not be the next senator of magic."

With a harrumph, Trina zipped up her bag. "Believe me, you don't want to get on that broomstick. If you don't like the politics now, you sure as hell won't like it there." Trina's phone buzzed, and she glanced down at it. "Oh, that's my brother. I'll see you later, okay?"

"Okay," I halfheartedly waved.

"And you better text me." She pointed a finger at me with a stern look. "And keep those lips off the boys!"

She laughed as she walked out the door, but I didn't join in. Trina might think my boy troubles were funny, but to me, they were the center of all my issues. I hadn't had this much drama since Jaron, and we all knew how that turned out. Maybe I should take a vow of celibacy? At least until I was done with college. I wasn't sure my GPA could handle any more incidents like at the mixer.

Which brought me to the other people I was avoiding. Not only did I have to hide from my fan club but from the guys who had nothing but Max on the brain. Or at least that was what it seemed like.

After the mixer, I got sparkling flowers from Ian. Chocolates that sang from Paul. Even Dale threw his hat into the ring with a note that transformed into a bird. It had been by far the most impressive of the three. However, I'd ignored every one of them. I had eaten the chocolates and saved the flowers. They sat on my nightstand now. The note from Dale was tucked in my drawer.

Those three weren't the only ones who had sent me gifts. Every guy in Winchester Academy had decided to tell me they suddenly wanted to date me. At least, that's what it seemed like. Never mind that the majority of them had never even met me let alone talk to me. They just wanted to get in good with the new power around campus.

I hadn't kept any of their gifts and had gone so far as to start rejecting them outright. I didn't need a whole horde of fanboys. I had my hands full with the guys I did like, never mind the ones I didn't even know.

I just hoped my grandparents didn't hear about any of this. It was just the kind of thing they would be all over. Or maybe appalled by. It was kind of hard to figure out how those two would react. The fact that they hadn't pushed me for anything after our first meeting. I hadn't even gotten so much as a text from them. I probably should get with them soon before they decided to take matters into their own hands.

"I see you haven't flown the coop yet. Still too scared to face the masses?"

I glanced up from the floor to where Ian leaned against my doorway his arms crossed over his chest and a sexy smirk on his lips. I offered him a weak smile. "Just working myself up to it."

"Well, I wouldn't wait too long." Ian moved away from the door and into the room. "They can smell fear."

I giggled. "Oh, is that right? I'll have to keep that in mind. Maybe get me an anti-ass-kisser charm. Think it'd work on you?" I arched a brow at him as he took the seat next to me on the bed.

Ian grinned. "Nah, don't lump me in with those idiots. They go where ever the power is. Now me? I like the diamonds in the rough. Those that have to be polished a bit to make them shine." Ian stroked my arm up and down, his face awfully close to mine.

"Oh? And you think I'm rough?" I murmured, not knowing why I was lowering my voice. Back away, Norman! Retreat, retreat. We just had this talk about kissing boys, and now you're already going back on it.

Before Ian could land one on me, I turned my face, making his lips graze my cheek. Clearing my throat, I rocked on the bed slightly. "So, what are you still doing here? Not going home for the holiday?"

Ian didn't even act like the fact that I had rejected him had bothered him. Knowing him, he probably just thought it made me more of a challenge. Instead, his nose crinkled up and his lips twisted into a grimace. "Let's see … spend time with a whole bunch of people who don't like my life choices and would do nothing but berate me for two weeks? Nah, I think I'll pass."

"Come on, it can't be that bad." I bumped him with my shoulder. "Paul will be there. I thought things were going better with you two?"

Lifting a shoulder, Ian didn't answer my question and even changed it back around to me. "What about you? Going home to the folks?"

I sighed and glanced at my empty bag. "Yeah, if I can ever get around to packing."

Ian's eyes followed mine and landed on the bag. "Pfft. That's a breeze." Without warning, he snapped his fingers and all my clothes piled into the bag in neat little piles. He'd even zipped it shut for me. "There! All done."

"Well, now what am I going to do until my parents get here? You took my one distraction away." I accused pretending to be annoyed.

A salacious grin covered Ian's lips as he leaned toward me. "Well, I could think of one thing." His fingers traced the side of my face, and I didn't have the strength to pull away from him this time.

"Maxine, I've been calling you for the past five minutes. Why haven't you answered your phone?" I jerked my face away from Ian at the sound of my mom's voice. "Oh, hello."

Ian smoothly turned away from me to greet my mom who stood by the door with a slight blush on her cheeks. Those Broomsteins, they even had the moms melting into puddles.

"I don't think we've met." Ian stood from my bed and sauntered over to my mom offering her a hand. "I'm Ian Broomstein. I'm a friend of your daughter's."

"A friend, are you?" Mom grinned at him and then looked to me. "Well, I'm so glad my daughter has found someone to spend her time with. I hope you are taking care of my girl?"

"When she lets me." Ian winked at me, and my mom giggled. Ugh, gag me.

"That's my daughter. Always the independent one. Well, it was nice meeting you, Ian. I hope to see you around." Mom patted him on the arm.

"Oh, I plan on it." He turned to me and grinned. "I'll see you around, Max. Don't forget, you still owe me that date."

Before I could get a word in, he was gone. Freaking Broomstein. Freaking hormones.

One thing was for sure. I needed a few weeks off just so I could get my head on straight.

"Man, if the guys in school were that fine when I was here, I might not have ever left." My mom fanned herself and approached me, a dreamy look in her eyes. "So, what's the story with him? Are you really just friends?"

I picked at the blanket beneath me. "I don't know yet. There are a few people I'm talking to, it's kind of hard to explain."

My mom's eyebrows shot up. "A few people? My, my, someone sure is popular."

I groaned and stood up, grabbing my bag from the floor. "Come on, let's just get out of here. I need a movie night and popcorn stat. And no mentioning Ian to dad." I warned my mom as she followed me out of my bedroom.

As we shoved our way through the crowded hallway, many of the students stopped to greet me. A few even tried to get some pictures with me which I slyly slipped out of with my mom watching silently beside me.

"And here I thought you weren't making friends." Mom clucked her tongue. "You have people falling all over themselves to talk to you. Anything you want to tell me?"

I winced and thought about what she might say about the whole ordeal with Sabrina. "Uh, it's a long story. I'll tell you

274

about it in the car." I slung my bag over my shoulder and started toward the front.

Who knew one simple kiss would cause so much trouble? I knew one thing was for sure. After winter break, these lips were staying exactly where they belonged. On the lip of a caramel macchiato.

My eyes caught onto Paul and Dale talking at the front desk on my way out. I ducked my head, my cheeks burning. Okay, maybe not just there. After all, this was college. If you couldn't let loose here, you couldn't do it anywhere.

Made in the USA
Columbia, SC
04 September 2018